Summer Escapes

Can you take the heat?

Love is in the air and the forecasts have promised a spell of sun, sea and sizzling romance. So let us whisk you away to this season's most glamorous destinations full of rolling hills, blissful beaches and piping hot passion! Take your seat and follow as these sun-kissed couples find their forever on faraway shores. After all, it's been said you should catch flights, not feelings— but who says you can't do both?

Start your journey to true love in...

The Venice Reunion Arrangement
by Michelle Douglas

Dating Game with Her Enemy
by Justine Lewis

The Billionaire She Loves to Hate
by Scarlett Clarke

Cinderella's Greek Island Temptation
by Cara Colter

A Reunion in Tuscany
by Sophie Pembroke

Their Mauritius Wedding Ruse
by Nina Milne

Fake Date on the Orient Express
by Jessica Gilmore

Available now!

Dear Reader,

Ever since I first picked up *Murder on the Orient Express*, the iconic train has seemed the epitome of glamour. So what better place to start a book that sweeps us from the opulent train to Venice, the Tuscan countryside and Chelsea in the height of summer? Add in a murder mystery weekend and a seriously competitive karaoke session and I had the perfect ingredients for a gorgeously summery opposites-attract, fake-relationship romance. I absolutely loved getting to know Lucas and Tally. He's a serious workaholic who doesn't have time for a relationship and she's a fun-filled, optimistic actress who refuses to be second best. I hope you love them as much as I do!

Love,

Jessica

FAKE DATE ON THE ORIENT EXPRESS

JESSICA GILMORE

Harlequin

ROMANCE

Harlequin® ROMANCE

ISBN-13: 978-1-335-47047-8

Fake Date on the Orient Express

Recycling programs for this product may not exist in your area.

Harlequin Enterprises ULC
22 Adelaide St. West, 41st Floor
Toronto, Ontario M5H 4E3, Canada
www.Harlequin.com

Printed in U.S.A.

Incorrigible lover of a happy-ever-after, **Jessica Gilmore** is lucky enough to work for one of London's best known theaters. Married with one daughter, one fluffy dog and two dog-loathing cats, she can usually be found with her nose in a book. Jessica writes emotional romance with a hint of humor, a splash of sunshine, delicious food—and equally delicious heroes!

Books by Jessica Gilmore

Harlequin Romance

Billion-Dollar Matches

Indonesian Date with the Single Dad

Blame It on the Mistletoe

Miss Right All Along

Fairytale Brides

Reawakened by His Christmas Kiss
Bound by the Prince's Baby

The Princess Sister Swap

Cinderella and the Vicomte
The Princess and the Single Dad

Winning Back His Runaway Bride
Christmas with His Cinderella
Christmas with His Ballerina
It Started with a Vegas Wedding

Visit the Author Profile page
at Harlequin.com for more titles.

For Rufus,
who has been the very best of good boys this year.

Praise for
Jessica Gilmore

CHAPTER ONE

TALLULAH JENKINS—TALLY TO her nearest and dearest—burst through the narrow door, put out a trembling hand to steady herself against the swaying of the train and announced dramatically, '*Zut alors!* Ze meestress. She is dead!'

The assorted group sitting around the long oval table looked up almost as one, their expressions a mix of surprise, unsuppressed excitement and, in a conspicuous couple of cases, disinterest. Their crystal glasses were half empty, their porcelain plates scraped clean. A wine waiter hovered in the background; another stood frozen in the act of clearing the plates.

'Dead?' A broad middle-aged man sprang to his feet. 'But how?'

'Stabbed!' Tally burst into loud sobs. 'Weeth 'er diamond letter opener!'

'Stabbed?' the man repeated, looking around to make sure everyone at the table had taken in this vital information. 'Come, *mademoiselle*, sit down and tell us all you know. We are stuck on this train until tomorrow and the telephones are cut off. If we don't apprehend this desperate villain now, he or she may get away scot-free—or we could all be murdered in our beds!'

The eight other people sitting at the table responded in different ways to this alarming news. One man, eyes already glittering with drink, merely motioned for his glass to be refilled, one pretty young woman continued to tap away at her anachronistic phone. A heavyset man just a few years older than Tally looked her up and down, his eyes lingering on her legs in a way that made her want to pull down her short black skirt as far as possible and wish her stockings weren't quite as sheer. Surely no real French maid would have worn an outfit that barely hit mid-thigh in the nineteen-twenties?

The rest of the group, however, entered into the spirit of the occasion and joined Hank, a Pinkerton's PI from Chicago—aka Neil, her employer—in cross-examining Tally who, between sobs, gasped out a tale of poison-pen letters, diamond thefts, secret liaisons and a conveniently dead much older husband who had left her murdered mistress a fortune, weaving in seven red herrings and one real clue. The key, Neil said, was to make the mystery difficult enough for them to have a real sense of achievement at solving the murder but simple enough to ensure they *did* solve it, especially when, like tonight, the murder took place against a backdrop of cordon bleu cooking and plenty of free and very expensive wine and unlimited spirits.

Finally, her interrogation over, Tally tottered to the door of the dining car, silk handkerchief to her eyes, uneasily aware that the heavyset man was tracking her every move. Intoxicated and entitled guests were always a risk at a gig like this, even in a venue as rarified as the Orient Express. She paused and turned, to take her scripted last dramatic look in the room, ready to deliver her final clue, only to meet the gaze of the man who sat at the head of the table. Impeccably dressed in a tuxedo Tally could tell was the real thing, tailored and made to measure, he had taken little part in the scene she had just starred in, but neither was he concentrating on drinking or leering. Instead, he was watching the other participants keenly. This must be Lucas West, the man rich enough to fund this entire extravaganza.

Tally held his gaze for a second too long, almost dropping character, feeling curiously more exposed under his assessing look than she did under the increasingly overly appreciative glances from his guest. Recollecting herself, she announced that she had found poison in Madame's belongings and, with a tremulous, appealing look at one of the more sober men—no need to encourage any of the others—that she was scared she wouldn't survive the night. Then out she tottered, shedding Cécile the second the dining car door closed behind her. She had, she reckoned, forty minutes to retire Cécile for now and change into Miss Wydenham, lady's companion and suspect number two, so she hastened through the two carriages of guest suites to the third carriage where she, Neil, Carmen and Freddie were being luxuriously accommodated alongside a couple of the guests.

Her compartment was unlike anything she had ever stayed in before. Opulent, cleverly designed, with all mod cons packaged in authentic vintage style. The comfortable sofa converted into a double bed and she had her own small breakfast table and dining chair. The wardrobe was just big enough to hold her several costumes, the tiny but utterly luxurious bathroom more than adequate for a change of hair and make-up. In fact, she had endured much smaller changing rooms and sleeping quarters when working in repertory theatre.

None of the troupe had expected to be staying in the luxurious en-suite accommodation, all more than happy with the historic twin cabins with shared bathrooms offered at a relatively lower price, but Lucas West had booked the dining car and three sleeping cars for exclusive use, which had meant a very welcome upgrade. Tally meant to enjoy every moment of it. Tomorrow night she would be sleeping in a five-star hotel in Venice before an evening flight home the following day, and then be handsomely paid for two days' work. It was a nice gig. But she thought as she stared at her make-up-free face in the mirror, it wasn't the gig she wanted.

She was thirty and still taking bit parts and commercial ventures like this, still aspiring to a career. In fact, she shouldn't be here right now. She should be in Croatia, on the set of what promised to be the next big fantasy franchise. She had been so close, down to the final two and she had absolutely killed it in the final auditions, she knew she had, but she had still lost out, to a girl nine years younger. It wasn't her first disappointment, not by a long way, but it felt like the most ominous. The role had felt like Tally's last chance. Now what? She wasn't sure she had many years of pulling off a French maid left. Then she would be the dowager, the long-suffering wife, the dowdy spinster.

But there was no time to dwell on that now. Briskly, she washed her face and redid her make-up, replacing the red mouth and long black lashes which characterised Cécile with a more demure look, putting on Miss Wyden-ham's tweed skirt and twinset, picking up a small bag which held a string of garnets and a pistol and with a sigh of relief pushed her squeezed feet into a rather nice pair of heeled brogues. She quickly brushed out her hair and re-pinned it, more severely than Cécile's, this time with no little perky cap. Her character brief was tidy, nondescript but with a hidden intelligence and a concealed beauty. Whatever that meant.

Tally took one last look at her script, making sure she had the clues right and her story straight, and left her suite. Just walking along the carriage was an adventure, with the beautiful wooden doors on one side opening into the suites, windows on the other showcasing the moving view as they travelled across France. The whole train was like a magical playhouse. If she had been a passenger she would have never tired of exploring, but these guests were evidently used to luxury on a grand scale, or not confident enough to show their excitement.

Another entrance, another scene, a few more dropped clues and several more red herrings, doing her best to convey a woman determined to present a demure front but unable to conceal occasional flashes of hidden fire, until her flustered exit after strategically dropping her bag and feigning shock at the spilled contents. Tally took a deep breath. One more scene and then she was free for the evening to enjoy her small but perfectly formed compartment.

It was a short but intensive trip. The train had left Paris in the late afternoon when, after everyone had settled into their compartments, the seeds of the mystery had been sown by Carmen playing the mysterious rich widow over cocktails and dinner. The murder had been timed for after dinner, with the rest of the evening taken up with various interviews and interrogations until a light late supper was served. The guests would then be free to go over the clues—or carry on drinking—before they too retired. Tomorrow the sleuthing would resume after breakfast with more interviews, more clues and an attempted murder or two before the afternoon summing up and solving of the case, leaving time for afternoon tea before the train reached Venice in the early evening. Tally just hoped the guests chose their culprit correctly, she didn't want her wrong character to be summoned to face justice. The downside of playing multiple parts.

Okay, time for Lucia, the murdered woman's niece, ward and probable heiress. She shimmied into the flapper dress which she had loved at the costume fitting but was now wishing was a little less tight and a little less short. Even in her frumpy-with-hints-of-sassy secretary's garb she'd found the man who had been overly interested in her maid's persona had made her feel uncomfortable. What he was going to think when he saw her in this little—very little— black dress she didn't want to imagine, especially if he kept drinking at the rate he had so far. Tally had been raised in a pub, she was more than comfortable taking care of herself, but this was a small, enclosed place, she was working and he was the guest of someone who was paying a lot, a really big lot, more than Tally could fathom, for his entertainment. Which meant a carefully aimed knee really had to be the very last resort.

She managed to avoid any eye contact with the drunker guests when she sashayed in, cigarette holder in one hand, rope of pearls in the other, to breathlessly deny any relationship with the murdered woman's latest lover, allowing herself to be tripped up by the detective's questioning. Instead, she concentrated on a woman of her own age who was obviously taking the whole murder mystery brief seriously, from her gorgeous beaded dress and hairband to a notebook full of observations. At one point Tally moved and found herself making eye contact with Lucas West again, her pulse speeding up as she met cool blue eyes. Rich and handsome, that was an unfairly devastating combination. She couldn't help allowing Lucia to flirt a little, batting her eyes in his direction, enjoying his reluctant almost smile back, surprisingly disappointed when with a muttered excuse he slipped away, hand already drawing his phone out of his pocket.

But throughout the scene she was aware that the leering man was even more fixated on her than before, his eyes running over her as if he could see through the sequins and fringes and tight support garment which had been the only way this dress had gone over her hips. The dress designer had clearly not got the loose fit flapper dress memo. She was really glad when she could deliver the last line and make her overly dramatic exit.

Ouch. As soon as she was alone Tally leaned against the wall and rubbed her heels. The high heeled, crystal buckled shoes were very cute but once again half a size too small. She considered kicking them off but wanted to get back to her room and enjoy a much-deserved long shower and room service as soon as possible so instead she pushed off the wall and hobbled along the corridor, opening the door to the next car, pausing as she heard the dining car door open and close and footsteps tap behind her. Damn, back into character again, Lucia would never allow shoes to beat her. She straightened and took a painful step when a voice slurred, 'Hey, wait.'

Tally's heart sped up. She'd been followed and now she was going to have to find a firm but diplomatic way to tell Mr Wandering Eyes to keep his hands and eyes to himself. Or maybe she could get to her compartment before he caught up—but there were two connecting doors and another full carriage to go before she was safe and he was gaining on her fast she could tell, even though she didn't dare to look around. Didn't want to indicate she could hear him.

'Hey, you with the legs, wait up.'

You with the legs.

With lines like that, it was no wonder the man

was chasing actresses down corridors. Tally stepped into the next carriage, letting the door swing shut behind her and trying to quicken her pace. Why hadn't she taken her shoes off? But if she had stopped to do that, he might have cornered her in the previous corridor and she would have felt more vulnerable with a bare foot.

Although she was feeling pretty darn vulnerable now.

At that moment a door to her left opened and Tally saw a tall broad figure standing there. Acting on an instinct she couldn't explain, she swerved in and threw her arms around the man's neck.

'Play along,' she murmured against his neck, surprised that she was able to notice even at a time of high stress that her hopeful saviour smelt really good, expensive yet tasteful and somehow sexy.

Not now, Tally.

'I've missed you,' she said, loudly enough for the man still lumbering up the corridor to hear.

There was an excruciating pause. Was she about to be summarily evicted from the room? Sacked? Cost Neil his lucrative luxury train murder mystery contract? Or would the man misinterpret what was going on here? That wouldn't be difficult with the skimpy dress and the embrace and all.

'I... I've missed you too?' Thank goodness. This guy clearly hadn't trained at drama school with many hours of improv, but she would take what she could get.

At that moment the drunken man stopped, his large body filling the narrow doorway. 'Here you are... Oh!' Tally couldn't bear to look round but she could imagine the knowing look on his face and cringed. 'I get it. Three's a crowd. You're a lucky man, West. I noticed her as soon as we boarded. Nice work.'

West? Oh, *fiddlesticks*. Of all the rooms on all the train, she had had to choose the one belonging to the client. How unprofessional was that?

Then, to her relief, her pursuer was gone. Tally knew she needed to let go, step back and apologise to Lucas West, but to her surprise her legs felt boneless. The only thing keeping her upright was the solid torso she leaned against and the arms that were somewhat gingerly holding her up.

'Sit down.' Lucas West's voice was low, a little gravelly and reassuring, as she was lowered onto a sofa. Tally noticed somewhat dimly that the suite was bigger and even more luxurious than hers. There was a separate sitting space, a permanent bed at the other end, already made up. A round table sat next to the window with a couple of glasses and a decanter set on a tray, more drinks and glasses in shelves behind it. Like her room, the walls were glossy walnut inlaid with gold, the green velvet décor both soothing and extravagant. 'You need a drink.' A whisky was shoved into her hand and her fingers automatically closed round it. 'You are in no state to work tonight. I'll let your boss know.'

'No, no, don't do that. The show must go on and I've dealt with men much more tenacious than him. Besides, my scenes are done for the night. I'm sorry, I'm not usually so easily spooked. I'm not sure what came over me.'

'No, I can only apologise for the behaviour of someone whose presence here I am responsible for. Please believe me when I say that Mr Johnson will be sorry for his behaviour at some point very soon.'

'I'm sure it would have been fine.' What was she doing, excusing his associate's behaviour? 'Like I say, I don't usually panic. He just seems to have had a lot to drink…' She trailed off.

The man's lips thinned. 'Which is no excuse. Are you sure you're okay?'

'Absolutely fine. Honestly. I'm done for the

night and am planning to enjoy my very lovely room and the very attentive room service before going over tomorrow's scenes. Hopefully, your...' friends? colleagues? associates? She wasn't entirely sure what this very extravagant private corporate event actually was. '...the rest of your party are busy solving the clues in there. There are some keen sleuths determined to work it out.'

'I'm glad.' But he didn't look glad. He looked thoughtful and more than a little annoyed. Not with her, Tally was pretty sure. But she knew that the drunken man would have cause to regret his behaviour. A shiver of something primal shivered through her. She wasn't the kind of woman who looked for a protector, but she had to admit it was rather nice for once to feel taken care of.

'Anyway, thank you again.' She put down her undrunk whisky and stood up. 'I'll let you get back to your guests. Happy detecting. Cécile, Miss Wydenham and Lucia will see you tomorrow.'

He didn't smile, just nodded, clearly still lost in thought, but she felt a frisson shiver through her as she slipped out of the still open door and limped down the corridor to her own carriage.

'Don't get too used to playing the damsel in

distress, Jenkins,' she told herself firmly. Like
all parts it was fun for a moment, but not reality. After tomorrow she would never see her
rescuer again.

Lucas West watched the actress make her exit,
her fresh floral scent lingering in the air. He
should thank her; he'd had his doubts about
Hunter Johnson from the start but couldn't put
his finger on why. Good to know his gut was
to be trusted. For a moment there his temper
hadn't been. He would have quite liked to pin
the lecherous weasel up against a wall. Not that
the girl—woman—needed him to. It had been
a masterly played diversion, although one that
could easily have backfired.

Right, time to return to the group before
Johnson spread his story and endangered the
actress's reputation for nothing more than a moment's gossip. Maybe he should have a quick
word with the murder mystery director, make
it clear the actress wasn't at fault. He turned on
his heel, only for his phone to ring again. He
checked the caller ID before answering. 'Felix?'

His tension dissipated at his brother's amused
tone. 'How's it going, Poirot?'

'You were right. This is a fascinating psycho-
logical experiment, apart from anything else.'

When his brother had suggested they take the family majority shareholders of Vineyard, the iconic preppy clothing company they were trying to buy, on a murder mystery jaunt on one of the world's most iconic trains, Lucas had deduced his brother was out of his mind. It was obscenely expensive and insanely decadent. But Felix had argued that there was nothing like the combination of alcohol, competitiveness and out of this world experience to show how someone really ticked. And he was right. Which was why Felix was usually the people person. It was unfortunate that a nasty dose of flu had meant he hadn't been able to come too, leaving Lucas to schmooze alone.

He might not be his brother but, hopefully, the goodwill generated by the trip alongside the above market price he was offering for their shares meant at least two guests would sell to them—and then WGO would be the Vineyard majority shareholder and which of the current board remained would be solely up to him.

Speaking of which. 'Johnson will be straight out,' he said curtly.

'Not surprising. His dossier is quite something.'

'There's something about Brianna Wu. She definitely has the right combination of people skills and intellect we need. I could see her as CEO. The rest need more analysis, so I'd better head back. I'll report further when we get into Venice tomorrow evening, but let's have those offers ready to go as soon as we are done here. I'll call tomorrow.'

'Look forward to it. Are you heading straight home tomorrow?'

'I'm spending a couple of days in Venice to carry on negotiating and then I've got some time booked in with Roberto; it made sense seeing as he's in Tuscany at the moment.'

'Work or play?'

'I've told him it's work, but, in reality, it's neither.' Lucas sighed. 'I'm a little worried about him, to be honest. I'm glad he's left England; the damp spring didn't do his chest any good at all.'

Roberto Leonardi was Lucas and Felix's late father's godfather, Lucas's mentor and his business partner during the last fifteen years as Lucas had transformed the small old-fashioned clothing manufacturer and retail chain his father had bequeathed him into a major fashion, design and retail powerhouse. Losing their father while still in their teens had been a shock for both boys, but Roberto had stepped in unobtrusively and sensitively, personally as well as corporately. Lucas owed him a debt that could never be repaid.

'Be careful.' He could hear the laughter in Felix's voice. 'I have it on good authority that the *bella* Isabella has joined him in Tuscany and you know what that means…' His brother whistled a few notes that were just about recognisable as the wedding march.

'No care needed. She's safely engaged to that *conte*. Thank goodness.'

Roberto had never accepted that Lucas owed him. After all, as an investor, WGO's success had benefitted him as well. But Roberto had always hoped that his oldest friend's grandson and his beloved granddaughter Isabella would make a match of it, bring the two families together, and Isabella had made it clear on several occasions that she was not at all averse to the idea. As a result, the announcement of her engagement six months ago had come as a huge relief. Lucas might feel indebted to Roberto and love the man almost as a father but that did not mean he wanted to be shackled to a spoilt heiress whose only interests were shopping and influencing.

'Oh…' Felix barely suppressed the glee in his voice. 'Haven't you heard? The engagement is off, which means *la bella* Isabella is back on the market. Summer in Tuscany, what could be more romantic?'

'Dammit.' Now that was awkward. Roberto hadn't looked at all well the last time Lucas had seen him, which meant it was going to be difficult to wriggle out of well-meaning suggestions that Lucas entertain his granddaughter while the older man took it easy.

It wasn't that Lucas wasn't capable of standing up for himself, he just didn't want to distress his well-meaning mentor more than he had to. It would be different if he was in a relationship, but he wasn't even casually dating at the moment. He'd grown up with a never present father who had neglected the family business and his family to enjoy an eventful love life; there was no way Lucas was repeating the same mistakes. His personal life could wait until WGO felt unassailable and he could afford to split his time between work and pleasure.

He said goodbye to a far too cheerful if still croaky Felix, then pocketed his phone and made his way back to the restaurant car, where he continued to watch and listen to the heated conversations as clues were analysed and witness statements scrutinised.

The evening continued, a mixture of drinking and sleuthing finishing with an excellent late-night supper which brought the night to a conclusion. Lucas lingered to say goodnight to his guests, glad when he could return to the solitude of his suite. Unlike the majority of his guests, he had barely drunk anything throughout the evening and so, after loosening his bow tie and shrugging his jacket off, he settled down with his laptop to get through some of his outstanding emails.

But it was hard to concentrate. Not because he was tired, he was used to long hours and late nights, but because he kept remembering the feel of a tall, gently curved body pressed up to his, felt the whisper of breath against his ear as the actress exhorted him to play along, saw the bravado in long-lashed brown eyes as she made out the incident was no big deal, even though he had felt her heart hammering against his.

Lucas raked his hand through his hair. 'Idiot,' he muttered.

It had been too long since his last relationship had come to a sticky end. Madeleine had not just known but sung along to his score, too busy herself at first to be interested in anything other than being asked and asking for an occasional plus-one, the odd dinner date and the occasional shared night. But after a few months she had become more demanding, unhappy when he had declined an invitation, started to suggest spending days and even weekends together. Lucas had liked her, been attracted to her, but hadn't been interested in anything more serious, and although he wasn't deluded enough to think he had broken her heart, he knew he had bruised her pride. Hurting her had never been his intention. He was angry with himself for missing the signs and allowing things to progress so far, and so he'd decided to take a dating hiatus, asking old friends to accompany him when he absolutely needed a plus-one.

Single life usually wasn't a problem, he was too busy to even notice most of the time, so why was he so unsettled tonight? It was probably the thought of Isabella free and single and Roberto playing hopeful matchmaker with no *conte* as shield.

It was a shame he had no shield of his own. Unless…no. Ludicrous.

But Lucas couldn't help opening the printed brochure detailing the trip's itinerary, his eyes drawn immediately to the cast information, a little paragraph detailing the history of the company and then four profiles, complete with pictures. There she was. Tally Jenkins. Dark eyes, a mass of wavy chestnut-brown hair, an amused expression smiling out. Quick-thinking, convincing, able to play multiple parts…

She would make an excellent shield. Not that there was any way he could ask her. And even if he did, it was unlikely she would agree. But as Lucas finally settled down to sleep in the surprisingly spacious bed, he couldn't help dwelling on how the answer to his immediate problem might be right here. If only it wasn't such a ridiculous idea.

CHAPTER TWO

TALLY ENJOYED AN excellent sleep in her comfortable bed, followed by an equally excellent breakfast, served on the small table by a smiling young man in a smart uniform that looked, like everything else, as if it came from the nineteen-twenties. She watched the mountainous views flash past through the window as she tucked into perfectly poached eggs on ambrosial toast, berries and whipped yogurt and then a selection of pastries she didn't exactly need but definitely wanted, before readying herself for the first scene of the day.

The day passed quickly. She managed to ignore the knowing looks from the man who had frightened her yesterday and did her best not to react to Lucas West, no longer dressed in black tie but a devastating linen suit that set his honed body off to perfection. Everyone looked better in nineteen-twenties costumes, she decided, the tailoring and cut flattering everyone.

She managed not to think about the events of the night before whilst in character and it wasn't until the clues had been solved, a denouement enacted and bows taken that she had the opportunity to consider possible consequences. She had been horribly unprofessional last night. This might not be a usual gig for her, but she was asked to work with Neil enough to make it a semi regular and lucrative income. She'd hate to lose out because of a simple mistake like launching herself at the client. She needed to apologise to Lucas for gatecrashing like that.

But how? When? She couldn't exactly approach him in front of any of the guests but he was never alone and Venice was rapidly approaching. The guests would be met on arrival by private cars and whisked away to a luxury resort for a night or two. Not that the actors could complain, they were also being treated to a night in the famous city, although their return the following evening would be on the kind of budget airline she doubted Lucas West and his guests even knew existed.

Now they were nearing Venice the guests and actors, including Tally, changed back into normal clothes, and they all gathered back in the dining car for final thanks. It was odd seeing the guests as herself, no longer in vintage dress but her smartest pink linen trousers and a white blouse with the kind of puffed sleeves that would have gladdened Anne Shirley's heart. She was aware the whole time of Lucas West, the watchfully quiet centre of a talkative group, and every now and then she felt his eyes rest on her, a thoughtful expression on his face making her shift uncomfortably.

Tally found herself in conversation with the youngest female guest, who had modelled a little and was hoping to break into acting, and although she looked for a moment to try and get Lucas West alone, there was no opportunity. By the time the train came into the station and their luggage had been loaded into the taxi he had disappeared, and her chance had disappeared with him. She gnawed her lip, thinking furiously. Should she say something to Neil herself? But Lucas West hadn't seemed angry, not with her anyway. Maybe she was worrying over nothing.

Her indecision was soon forgotten as the water taxi sped them up the Grand Canal to their hotel. It was Tally's first time in the famous city and she was soon overcome by the sights, sounds and smells. It was exactly like she had dreamed it would be only more vibrant, much busier. She was soon snapping away, sending a quick selfie to her mother and step-dad with a Wish you were here. Her mother responded with a photo of the beer delivery for that day waiting to be unpacked and a laughing crying emoji.

The small troupe were staying in an upmarket chain. It didn't take long to check in and shower before meeting for a meal but although Tally was desperate to explore by the time they had eaten it was past ten and so she decided to get up early and make the most of the next day before her late flight. She excused herself right after dinner and went straight to bed, setting her alarm for a wincingly early hour.

Sure enough, she was up and out by seven, after donning a hat and a pair of sunglasses along with the trousers and top she'd worn the evening before. She'd kept her make-up down to sunscreen and mascara along with a bright red lipstick. Her mother wasn't one for dishing out loads of advice but one thing she always did say was there was nothing like a dash of lipstick, as armour, to finish off an outfit or to cheer you up and Tally had soon realised it was true. Whether her mother's wisdom came from her long dead acting career or from being a pub landlady for the last twenty-five years Tally wasn't sure, but it was good advice. She quickly messaged the murder mystery chat to say she was off to explore and slipped away. She liked the rest of the actors, and was grateful for the job, but they weren't the people she would choose to spend time with on her first visit to Venice.

Her steps took her first to St Mark's Square. It was, just like the water taxi up the Grand Canal, almost achingly familiar, with the palace dominating one end and restaurants with tables set up amongst the rows of pillars already hosting some early breakfasters. Tally hadn't eaten so, preparing herself for what she knew would be an exorbitant bill, took a seat and ordered coffee and toasted brioche with eggs and sat back and people watched.

The square was mostly empty when she sat down, but over the next hour started to get busier and busier. She knew this was nothing, that the famous tourist destination would soon be crammed—the travel guide she had read had suggested getting there very early or in the evening after the cruise ships and day trippers had left. Glad that she had managed to enjoy it whilst quiet she paid the bill, managing not to wince at the price, and slipped away down a side street.

It was surprising how easy it was to return

to solitude; she was just a couple of streets—
or canals—away from the tourist areas and she
almost had the historic city to herself. Lost in
a daydream of colour and beauty, Tally wan-
dered narrow paths alongside narrow canals,
making friends with cats and exploring shops
selling everything from high end jewellery to
expensive stationery to the ubiquitous masks.
The actress in her was enthralled by the masks
and she was sorely tempted by a simple carnival
one which only covered the eyes. It was delicately decorated with black and gold swirls and
fastened with a black velvet ribbon. She held it
up to her face and stared at herself in the mirror, charmed by how instantly it transformed
her, made her mysterious. But the price tag was
far more than she could justify and reluctantly
she went to return it.

'You should buy it.' The voice, low and gravelly and assured, quivered through her and Tally
turned quickly, the mask still in her hands. 'It
suits you.'

Lucas West was dressed in the immaculate
grey linen suit he'd worn yesterday despite the
heat of the day which saw most other tourists
in jeans and T-shirts, but somehow he looked
cool, unruffled. His dark, almost black hair was
ruthlessly combed back, but one strand had re-

belliously slipped over his forehead, softening
the hard angles of his face, the darkness of his
hair a stunning contrast to his blue eyes.

'Mr West!'

Of all the mask shops in Venice he had to
walk into hers. But that was good, wasn't it?
She had wanted a chance to apologise.

'Lucas, please.'

'Lucas.'

Ugh, now why did she sound so breathless?
Yes, he was undeniably gorgeous—and why
should she deny it? It was an objective state-
ment, just like saying Venice was gorgeous, or
the mask was gorgeous, but neither of those
made her knees suddenly weaken and the breath
leave her chest.

She looked at the mask. 'I love it, but I don't
need it.'

Damn it, now she sounded wistful.

'And you only buy what you need?'

'I try to. Good for the planet and the bank
balance.' Plus, when one had moved back into
one's childhood bedroom over a pub after a
bad breakup, space for belongings was at a pre-
mium.

Lucas studied her, frowning. 'You should
have it,' he said. 'Let me buy it for you. As a
thank you gift for your work yesterday.'

'You already paid us and put us up in a hotel here,' she protested. 'I think most people would consider a night on the Orient Express and a night in Venice more than enough of a thank you.'

The corner of his mouth twitched but he didn't reply, just held out his hand for the mask. Tally shifted, unsure. It was difficult to argue with someone who didn't reply. Her only real options were to agree or to put the mask down and walk out of the shop. The latter might be a more principled stance but felt rude.

'Please,' he said, low and coaxing, and Tally couldn't help but laugh, although half in exasperation.

'It's not necessary, but if you insist,' she said, handing him the mask and reminding herself that he was so rich he had just hired out part of the most famous train in the world. 'But I must buy you a drink to say thank you. There's something I had hoped to talk to you about anyway and didn't get the opportunity before. Bumping into you like this is serendipitous.'

'Serendipitous,' he echoed. 'Funny, that was exactly the word I was looking for.'

Lucas hadn't set out to find the actress—Tally. He'd still been mulling over his crazy idea when they disembarked and when she had disappeared it had felt like the answer to his unspoken question. But bumping into her felt like fate. And her offer of a drink even more so.

They left the small shop in silence, Tally clutching her paper bag, but she gave a rapturous sigh as they stepped out into the small alley.

'It's rare to visit somewhere that's exactly how you hoped it would be but even more so, don't you think?' she said.

'First time in Venice?' Lucas asked.

'First time in Italy, to my shame. I wish I had more time here, not that I'm complaining,' she added hurriedly. 'I am very grateful for the hotel and the opportunity to explore. How about here?'

Here was a small café restaurant next to the mask shop. Like so many cafés in Venice it had a small, windowless interior, dominated by a large, curved bar, the majority of the tables and chairs set up outside.

'Fine, what would you like?'

'I'm paying, remember. What would *you* like?'

Lucas sat down somewhat cautiously on a rickety chair. The street was narrow, quiet, the view mostly the walls of the street with a glimpse of canal at the end, but Tally seemed delighted with her choice.

'I much prefer somewhere off the tourist trail, the kind of place locals use, don't you?'

Did he? Lucas travelled a lot but usually he was entertaining and the restaurant was picked by his PA, or he would grab a quick bite alone, often in the hotel or somewhere nearby. But she was right. The coffee smelt delicious and the location was as peaceful as Venice in late June got.

Tally thanked the waiter as he set down the coffees and took a sip of hers, before biting her lip. 'So, like I said, I'm glad I ran into you, and not just because you were absurdly generous and bought me a mask.' Her eyes were hidden by her sunglasses, her straw hat low on her forehead, but her cheeks were pink and her voice more than a little self-conscious. 'I wanted to apologise.'

That was unexpected. Lucas sat back. 'Apologise? Why?'

'It was really unprofessional of me to deal with that situation the other night the way I did. I put you in an awkward position. I'm very grateful you didn't report me to Neil, but I just wanted you to know that I don't usually go around embracing clients. I should have…'

He held up a hand to cut her off. 'No, I'm sorry. Sorry that a guest of mine put you into that situation. I hope it goes without saying that there will be consequences, but you absolutely do not owe me an apology or need to second-guess any decision you made.'

'That's... Thank you.'

Lucas took another sip of his really excellent coffee and assessed her discreetly. Her mass of hair was pulled back into a ponytail underneath the hat, but what he could see was a chestnut-brown, streaked through with natural-looking blonde and coppery highlights, glossy and shiny. She had an expressive face, with high cheekbones and a dimple at the side of her full mouth. Her linen trousers and white top looked fresh and classy, the red lipstick adding a touch of style. She clearly had manners, was quick on the uptake, knew how to play a part...

'Do you have another mystery booked after this?'

She shook her head. 'Not for me. I'm not a regular member of the company but I fill in when needed. Pritti, who usually plays the roles I did, was at a family wedding this week so Neil asked me to cover.' She laughed. 'It wasn't a hardship. I've done it before, and when he told me that in addition to the fee I'd get a night on the famous Orient Express and a night in Venice I wasn't exactly going to say no!'

'Must be interesting, being an actress.'

'At times, but it's an insecure world. I actually spend more time behind the bar of my mum's pub than I do on stage or screen, but when it works out it's glorious.'

'And what's next?'

'Auditions, I guess.' Her mouth twisted and she paused for a moment. 'Actually, I don't have anything lined up so bar work it is, I suppose. At least I'm lucky to have that.'

Which meant she was free for the next few weeks.

'Tally is an unusual name. Is it a stage name?'

'All mine, short for Tallulah. My mother's first professional role was in *Bugsy Malone* and I was named in homage to that. I always thought it could be worse. She could have played…oh, I don't know… Goneril or Titania, and then where would I be?'

'Tallulah.' It suited her. 'It's unusual enough to mean you didn't need a stage name, I suppose.'

'Yep. Small mercies.'

She had finished her coffee and sat back, looking around the street as if it was the most beautiful of surroundings and not a nondescript alley in an unfashionable part of Venice. 'I'm glad we got a chance to clear the air. And thanks again for the mask, but this city won't explore itself and I need to be back at the hotel to grab my things and leave for the airport for five. What are your plans?'

'Does head back to the hotel and tackle my emails before a business meeting with some of yesterday's guests sound really dull?'

She laughed. 'I mean, it's an option. Not as much fun as trying every water taxi to see where I end up and wandering around hidden corners, but each to their own.'

She was an off-the-beaten-track kind of tourist. It figured.

'Tallulah Jenkins, would you have dinner with me tonight?'

The words were out before he could stop them. Throughout this chance meeting Lucas had been telling himself that his idea was a mad one, but the more time he spent with her, the more it seemed plausible. She needed a job; he needed a way to keep Roberto happy. It could work.

'Dinner?' Thanks to the sunglasses, he couldn't tell if she was excited or horrified by the suggestion, her voice gave nothing away.

'No expectations. Not a date.' Ouch, that was

awkward. It was a good thing Felix wasn't here to hear this mangled attempt at whatever this was.

'Not a date, got it.' Was she laughing at him? Understandable if so, that had been the opposite of smooth.

'Not that you are not dateable, but I'm not looking for anything like that right now.' What *was* he doing? Some negotiator. 'Just dinner, a chance for you to explore some more of this city.'

'Obviously, that would be lovely.' She didn't sound wholly convinced but he couldn't blame her for that. 'Thank you for asking, but I'm flying back this evening.'

'To bar work? I mean, do you have to rush back? I could ask my PA to change your flight and extend your stay.'

'I couldn't ask you to do that.'

'You're not,' he pointed out. 'I'm asking you. And I know it seems a little unorthodox, and I don't blame you for being wary, but there's possibly something… I just need to think about it. But I understand if you want to get back.' In fact, it might be easier all round, especially now he had made such a hash of asking her.

'I…' She was clearly undecided but then

seemed to come to a decision. 'No, actually another day here would be lovely. Thank you.'

'Great, let me have your number and I'll send you some details about this evening and my PA will take care of the rest. Thank you, Tally.'

There, no decisions, no irreversible offers made, but the possibility was still there. This evening could be a sort of unofficial audition, a trial to see how at ease in each other's company they could be, if he would want to spend a week in her company—and vice versa.

Who knew, if it worked out then maybe it could be a longer-term arrangement, for the rest of the year? He had a few weddings and business events to attend and his female friends were nearly all coupled up and too busy to attend anything but the most unusual or luxurious events with him. He wasn't a superstitious man but Lucas couldn't help but think that fate had sent him Tallulah Jenkins for a reason and he would be an idiot not to take advantage of that.

CHAPTER THREE

TALLY CONTINUED TO explore but it was hard to throw herself into sightseeing when her mind was going over and over the conversation she had just had, and the bizarre outcome of it. Had she really agreed to stay in Venice for an extra night in order to have dinner with a handsome and rich man which was explicitly not a date but for some unspecified reason? Like what? What would Lucas West want with a some-time actress stroke barmaid? Would she feel more excited if it *was* a date? She was out of practice, it was true, too bruised for too long to throw herself back into the bearpit that was modern dating.

At that moment a message popped up on her phone from Candace at WGO, confirming that her hotel stay had been extended and that she just needed to message with her preferred flight home and it would be confirmed for her. Wow, life really was different for the rich. Tally quickly messaged Neil to let him know she was planning to stay on for another day or so and then set about exploring some more, determined to stop wondering what the evening had in store and to make the most of this unexpected opportunity. Maybe, if her return flight was an open one, she wouldn't need to return to London immediately. She quite fancied heading out to the islands, exploring further afield. She wouldn't be able to afford her hotel, of course, but there must be a hostel somewhere for the more budget minded traveller.

Lunch was toasted ciabatta stuffed with cheese and vegetables, more ambrosial coffee and then a mid-afternoon gelato to keep her going. It had been far too long since she had last had a holiday. Not since, well, not since Max, and that had been a rainy week in the Lake District which had been more mud than sunshine. Tally waited for the usual sweep of pain and loss to hit her, but for the first time in eleven months she didn't physically recoil at the thought of her ex, she just felt sad. Sad that it had ended so brutally, sad that she hadn't seen it coming.

No, she was *not* thinking about Max right now. She took her gelato along a hidden canal, the houses on either side crammed together, rising above her three or four storeys high, peeling and faded and shuttered and full of hidden mysteries. She walked to the end and stood looking out to sea at the afternoon sun dancing off the swell of the waves. What a magical, impossible place this city was. And here she was, free to explore and enjoy it. No ties, no responsibilities, no reason to rush back. Maybe she had been looking at this all wrong. Instead of bemoaning her broken relationship, her move back above the pub, the loss of Max, she should turn it all around. She was free. No responsibilities. No rent. No one would bat an eye if she said she was going to head off to the Lakes, to Verona, to Florence after this. She could. Maybe she even would.

Maybe.

Her phone lit up with a message, another from Candace, confirming arrangements for that evening. She was to meet Lucas at eight, at a vaporetto stop close to her hotel. Dress code: smart.

That might be a slight issue. She had three costumes in her borrowed case but she didn't think an overly short and tight flapper dress met the brief, although it was smarter than the maid's outfit. Her own bag only contained a T-shirt to sleep in, the crumpled dress she had worn to board the train and a pair of shorts, a T-shirt and a hoodie. Why hadn't she inherited her mother's pack rat genes? Charlene Jenkins never went anywhere without an outfit for every conceivable and inconceivable occasion. She would absolutely have packed something suitable for a smart dinner with a handsome millionaire just in case.

Tally had limited time and an equally limited budget but found a couple of high street chains in the busier part of the city and, blessing the early summer sales, managed to pick up a silky green slip dress and a pair of jewelled sandals with a matching bag, spending the rest of her budget on a beautiful bronze throw from one of the many market stalls. A shower, a hair wash and a wrestling match with the hotel hairdryer later and she had to admit she looked quite nice. The heat and humidity demanded she indulge her waves rather than tame them so, with a liberal use of sea salt spray, she coaxed them into some order before spending some time on her make-up, elongating her eyes and lashes before adding her usual dash of red lipstick.

She took a step back and surveyed herself cautiously. Not bad. The green of the dress and the bronze wrap enhanced her brown eyes and she was optimistic that the sandals weren't going to pinch. Thank goodness she had had a pedicure before coming away. She would do.

She carried that confidence with her as she left her hotel and made her way through the evening crowds to the vaporetto stop, adding her sunglasses as protection against the still bright setting sun. A good costume wasn't essential for the confidence to inhabit a character, that was one of the first things Tally had learned at drama school, but it helped. What you needed was a core belief in who you were portraying, a deep-seated knowledge.

Tally Jenkins might not have expected to be heading out for dinner in Venice that night rather than being crammed into a too small seat on her budget flight home but she wasn't going to show it. She looked good and she knew it, an old hand at turning cheap outfits into couture with just a state of mind, and so she was poised and outwardly confident as she waited for Lucas, two butterfly clips holding her hair back from her face, wrap folded on her arm. But she still jumped when he spoke, too lost in the view to hear him approach.

'You look beautiful.'

Tally half turned, a little breathless, annoyed at being caught out. 'Thank you, so do you.' Another linen suit, this one a light blue, his shirt impossibly white, hair slicked back apart from that one rebellious lock, sunglasses that definitely cost more than her whole outfit. 'I mean...' so much for poised and in control '...you look good too.'

Ugh. Nice going, Tally.

To her relief, his mouth twitched with suppressed amusement. 'I'll gladly take either. Ah, here's our ride. Ready?'

'Absolutely.'

The boat he handed her into wasn't one of the public taxis. Instead, it was a private launch with polished and comfortably upholstered wooden seats, the pilot clad in a smart uniform. Two glasses and a bottle of champagne chilled in an ice bucket and a deep-sided bowl held crisps. Tally's stomach gurgled. That ice cream seemed a long time ago.

Also, how cool was this. Cool and maybe just a little OTT for something that apparently wasn't a date and carried no expectations. Obviously, Lucas was richer than Croesus, or so she assumed after the last few days, but even multi-millionaires could have ulterior motives. She glanced over as he expertly slit the foil on the champagne cork, popping it silently and efficiently as if he had popped a thousand champagne bottles before. Which he almost definitely had.

Champagne. A private boat. It might not be a date but was Lucas West trying to *seduce* her? Tally watched him pour the champagne, her eyes lingering on strong, corded wrists, moving up to fixate on the vee of his throat, tanned against the white of his shirt, and her pulse began to speed up, insistent and almost pleasurably painful. Would that be a bad thing? It had been far too long since she'd had sex and Lucas was undeniably attractive. Sexy even.

It wasn't that Tally hadn't had offers since Max had finished their relationship, or unceremoniously dumped her, depending on who she was talking to, but as she preferred to steer clear of actors and the rest of her would-be suitors were regulars at her mother's pub—although, to be fair, not all were twice her age; Leroy was at least three times—she hadn't taken any of them up. As for the apps, they were a depressing tragi-comedy of ghosting, lies and misrepresentation. If that was the best that was out there then Tally had reconciled herself to being alone. Maybe one day she could do one of those marrying herself ceremonies.

But if Lucas West *was* interested in her, even as a one-off, one-night thing, then maybe she could hold off on buying the dress. Tally Jenkins still had it, whatever *it* was.

Lucas handed her the glass of champagne and she took it with a smile. The pilot of the boat waited before Lucas sat down before setting off, so smoothly her champagne barely moved in the glass.

'Cheers.' She held her glass up to Lucas. 'And thank you for this treat.'

'You're welcome. Thank you for being so accommodating.' Lucas held his glass up to her then sat back, brow furrowed as if deep in thought.

Tally reassessed the situation. He wasn't *acting* like a seducer. He wasn't leaning in close, arm around the back of her seat, smiling into her eyes. If this wasn't a seduction, maybe it was a kidnapping. She had no idea where they were going after all. But then he wasn't acting like a kidnapper either. Not that she had any idea what a kidnapper acted like, outside of an episode of a police drama she'd had a two-minute bit part in the preview as the victim whose kidnap and murder the alcoholic disgraced ex-policewoman heroine had to solve.

'It's easy to be accommodating when you're being spoilt rotten. This whole gig has been extra special. It's going to be hard to return to the usual cycle of trying to get through to my agent and submitting videos after this.' She laughed. 'Not that I'm complaining, I chose this life after all.'

'Did you always want to be an actress? Or should I say actor?' Lucas asked.

'Either works. And no. Anything but.'

'That makes sense.' Oh, he looked even more handsome when he almost smiled.

'I know. I knew better, you see; my mother was an actress and she did her best to put me off.'

'Was she in anything I would have seen?'

'Not unless you were a soap addict in the mid-nineties?'

'Well, I was about five so not so much.'

'In that case, no, I doubt it. She had some bit parts as a child actor, then *Bugsy Malone* in the West End before getting her big break in her teens as the daughter of a new family on the street in *River Close*. For a while it looked like she was going to have a really big career. She won awards, was on the front of magazines, in the headlines, but by the time she was twenty-one it all started to fall apart. The role ended in true soap melodramatic style with a shoot-out, a hostage situation and a tragic death on the eve of her wedding, then she had me and finding work as a single mother proved harder than she'd hoped.'

It was always a relief when people hadn't heard of her mother. It meant they had no idea who her father was and she preferred it that way. It was so awkward when people remembered that old scandal. She could see them scanning her face for a resemblance to him, hungry for any nugget of gossip about his life. Not that she had any nuggets to drop. It was hard to have the inside information when you were so far on the outside you were practically in the Arctic Circle.

'And yet here you are. Despite your mother's warnings.'

'I must be a glutton for punishment. I went to university to study History but ended up spending all my time in the drama club. Then I auditioned for drama school, assuming I wouldn't get in and knowing if I did I couldn't afford it, but they gave me a scholarship. I got an agent on graduating and thought I had made it. That fate had big things in store for me. But eight years later here I am. Barmaid, occasional murder mystery participant, bit player on several early evening dramas, star of three commercials, repertory theatre veteran and survivor of one almost in the West End musical that closed in under a week. I promise myself every six months that I'm ready to walk away and yet somehow never do. How about you? Did you always want to be…?'

To be what? Young, hot and rich? Smooth arranger of hotels and flights—at least through his PA? Tally realised she had no idea what Lucas actually did.

'A businessman?'

Oh, that was lame. Really, really lame.

Lucas half shrugged. 'The business was founded by my great-great-grandfather. Like you, it's a family legacy, I suppose.'

Clearly a much more successful legacy than Tally's.

'To family legacies,' she said, holding her glass to his again. 'And how they get us in the end.'

'To family legacies,' he echoed. His expression was hidden behind his sunglasses, but for one moment Tally could have sworn that Lucas looked almost wistful.

Now they were here, Lucas wasn't sure how to broach his idea or even if he should. Objectively speaking, the whole thing was absurd. Besides, she probably had a boyfriend, something he should have checked before embarking on this madness. It wasn't like him to be so disorganised. Usually, a plan fell into place almost as soon as he thought about it, each step laid out like a path ready to be followed. This whole idea, on the other hand, was a chaotic and potentially embarrassing mess. But here they were, approaching the private island on which could be found Venice's most exclusive restaurant.

On a summer's night like this, most of the tables were set up al fresco, lit up by candles, discreet low lights and fairy lights twisted through trellises and trees. Tables were set at discreet distances, perfect for romance and assignations—or to ask an awkward question. Lucas glanced over at Tally, who was gazing on the scene with obvious delight. The setting sun cast a golden glow over her, eyes wide and full mouth parted as she exclaimed how gorgeous it all looked, and Lucas realised again what a beautiful woman she was. Which was good. Beauty was a costume of its own and it would be helpful for the role he had in mind.

The next few minutes were taken up with the usual business of greetings, being seated, menus handed over, specials relayed in appropriately respectful tones, water ordered. He'd barely touched the complimentary champagne from the boat, which now stood chilling in a bucket by the side of the table, the service so seamless he barely noticed it arrive.

He established that Tally ate fish not meat.

'I know,' she said laughingly. 'I'm a hypocrite but it works for me.'

She opted for vegetables prepared *de misto* to start, followed by the *risotto al nero*, an iconic Venetian dish in Venice which, the waiter assured her, was unsurpassed here.

Lucas ordered the same, food the furthest thing from his mind, then sat back and surveyed his companion. Unlike most of the women here, her dress was almost definitely not real silk, the stones glittering in her ears were not real diamonds, her sandals hadn't been handmade for her, but she wore the ensemble with such confidence she outshone them all. Her hair was loose, held back by pretty clips, the waves falling down her back, and her expression gave nothing away.

'So,' she said as the waiter finally moved away, choices noted, champagne poured. 'This is really lovely but I can't help wondering what it's all for. What do you want from me, Lucas West?'

Direct and to the point. He liked it. 'Does it have to be for anything?'

'Oh, yes.' She nodded solemnly. 'You barely know me, I'm not one of the guests you were trying to impress. We already did the apology dance and you bought me a mask so it's not about what happened a couple of nights ago.'

'A mask hardly makes up for the fact that you were intimidated whilst working for me.'

Lucas's tone was harsher than he had intended but he was still filled with rage when he remembered the slight quiver in her body as she had pressed herself against him, the shadow of fear in her eyes. He didn't usually believe that violence solved anything, but he bitterly regretted not aiming one perfect punch at Johnson's smug, repellent face. Knowing he'd get his revenge in the boardroom went some way to consoling him, but not far enough.

'And if this is a romantic evening…' She paused and looked around at a setting made for romance—or discretion—and bit her lip. 'It's all very beautiful but you don't need to pull out quite so many stops to impress me. Not that I'm not impressed, it's hard not to be.'

'I'm not trying to romance you,' Lucas said, although part of him wished it was that simple, a few days' dalliance with a beautiful woman in a beautiful city. He'd been single for far too long. Maybe it was time to forget how things had turned out with Madeleine and find another equally busy, equally as uninterested in long-term relationships woman who was after something mutually beneficial. 'I would like to employ you.'

Her brown eyes widened. 'Employ me? You…what…need a resident actress on-site? Or a resident barmaid? I *can* multitask.'

'No, but I do need a plus-one for the next week, and possibly, if it works out, over the next few months.' His mouth twisted as he thought of the several corporate events he had to attend and the couple of weddings cluttering up his diary.

'A plus-one?' Her brow furrowed and then she broke into a wide incredulous grin. 'Get out! You want me to be what…your fake girlfriend? How very nineties romcom of you. I love it!'

Lucas wasn't sure if the romcom reference was a good thing or not. 'Obviously, you would be paid for your part, and I would give you an allowance to ensure that you had all you need to play the part.'

Tally leaned forward, eyes sparkling. 'Depends what part you need. If I am Tally Jenkins, jobbing actress who you met on the Orient Express, then I have all I need, but if I am Tallulah Jenkins, society woman of mystery, then that could be very expensive indeed. Let me get this straight. You are asking me to pretend to be your plus-one…'

'Actually, I want you to pretend to be my new girlfriend,' he corrected her, and her smile widened.

'Girlfriend for the next week, possibly longer, and you are prepared to pay me and outfit me to do so. Why?'

It was a fair question. 'You are the right age, quick-thinking…' Should he say beautiful when this was a business arrangement? 'You know how to dress for myriad parts,' he said instead. 'You are an actress so used to pretending, and you said yourself you have nothing lined up. All I am doing is offering you a job.'

'Not one I can put on my CV,' she murmured. 'Well, that's all very clear, thank you. But I didn't mean why *me*. I get that for all the reasons you just said. But what I don't get is why *you*. Either you're a very convincing conman or you're on the serious side of rich. You're easy enough on the eye, don't seem to have any terrifying personality quirks, your hygiene seems okay, you can plan a seriously impressive evening out—surely you can get any woman you want without needing to draw up a contract?'

'Probably,' he admitted, and she laughed. 'But I need someone who isn't looking for hearts and flowers and a happy-ever-after, who won't be offended when I'm too busy to message or call, who doesn't need all my attention and is quite happy if they are left alone while I talk to clients or prospective partners. That kind of plus-one takes more finding than I have time for.'

Tally was leaning forward, pointed chin propped on one slender hand, regarding him with fascination. 'I can see that. Is that your usual type?'

'Usually, yes.'

'I see that you're not going to find the perfect woman immediately, but I still am surprised you need to employ one. You strike me as a pretty organised kind of guy. Surely you would have been aware you would need a plus-one before now?'

'The summer's events have been looming,' he admitted. 'But I received a piece of news yesterday that expedited matters. Tally, before I go any further, let me know if this sounds like an outrageous proposal and you have no intention of saying yes, and if so, we can put this aside, enjoy what promises to be an excellent dinner and return to Venice with no hard feelings.'

He sat back, champagne glass in hand, outwardly cool but, to his surprise, Lucas realised he wanted her to say yes. That he was enjoying her company. That he liked the way she questioned him, the amusement in her eyes. The fact he was attracted to her was beside the point. He didn't need attraction for the role he wanted her to play. In fact it complicated things.

'I haven't decided yet,' she said after a while. 'It's definitely not a yes, but it's not a no either.'

'That sounds fair.'

The waiter came over at that moment to refill their glasses and to bring them a plate of freshly baked bread with a saucer of delicious-smelling olive oil and a trio of tapenades.

He waited until Tally had enthusiastically helped herself to the bread and spooned a little of each tapenade and the olive oil onto the side of the plate before tackling her very pertinent question.

Why now?

'Have you ever heard the saying that it takes one generation to build a fortune, one to cement it and one to squander it?'

'It's not a saying often used in the pub, but yes.'

'Well, in our family it took one generation to move from the mill floor to mill owner, another two to grow the business to something established and lucrative and one to set about a managed decline. My father should never have been a businessman. He was happiest in London, at his friends' country estates or Mustique villas, throwing and attending parties, conducting a long string of love affairs. As for the business, it was at best unmanaged decline, at worst asset-stripping. When he died, he left behind a tangled personal life, a lot of debts and a business whose value seemed to be in what was left of its reputation and the property it was housed in. I was eighteen, Felix, my brother, fourteen.'

'Wow. I know a little what it's like to have an unsatisfactory parent. I'm sorry.'

He nodded in acknowledgement. 'Roberto was my father's godfather, my grandfather's best friend. We had been supplying his business with wool and other materials for years. And he said if I wanted to turn things around he would help me. He offered me a kind of apprenticeship so instead of university I headed to Milan, spending two years in every part of his business from shop floor to stockroom whilst studying remotely.

'Thanks to him, WGO is no longer known for catalogues in the back of Sunday supplements selling clothes that were old-fashioned fifty years ago but for in-demand high fashion. Our suits are worn by stylish successful men around the world and our women's fashion is expanding exponentially. Our wholesale business supplies brands all over the world. We turned around the retail business, keeping the bricks and mortar and finally expanding into online despite a difficult time for retail, acquiring brands, companies and manufacturers as we grow. The company hasn't just turned around, it's bigger, better and healthier than it ever has been and changing and growing all the time. That was the point of this trip. My guests are the last family shareholders in a US preppy clothing company I want to buy.

'But what I need you to understand is that Roberto gave me the tools I needed, the self-belief, and the capital when no bank would touch a failing business headed up by an eighteen-year-old novice and he was by my side the first few years. I owe him everything.'

He stopped. Lucas wasn't sure when he had last said so much in one go. But Tally didn't look bored, she looked fascinated.

'And I guess Roberto is the reason you're in desperate need of a plus-one.'

Lucas nodded. 'Not so much Roberto, but his Achilles heel. His granddaughter. Isabella.'

CHAPTER FOUR

TALLY HAD NEVER been anywhere like this. A restaurant on a private island in the middle of the Venetian lagoon, brought here by private boat with champagne laid on. It was the kind of life she imagined living if she ever made it, the kind of life her father wouldn't even blink at. And she could carry on living this kind of life for another week, for the rest of the summer if she said yes to Lucas West's surprising proposition.

She didn't know if she was disappointed or relieved that this wasn't a seduction attempt. It would be easier to say no but thank you if he wasn't quite so devastating. If he wasn't looking at her out of eyes a dark blue like the dusk lit sea, if she hadn't had the feeling that he had just revealed far more than he had intended, far more than the mere words he had said.

She knew what it was like to have a father figure instead of your own actual father. The need to keep proving yourself, to show your love and gratitude, the awareness that love might not be conditional but felt that way.

'So, let me guess.' She kept her tone deliberately light as the waiter set a plate filled with a delicately arranged feast of fresh vegetables so lightly battered and fried it was as if they had been plucked fresh from the earth in front of her and merely waved in front of a flame. 'Roberto thinks that a marriage between his best friend's grandson and his own beloved granddaughter would be the very thing to allow an old man to die happy but, much as you love him, for whatever reason that's a step too far?' She took a bite of a courgette and closed her eyes as she savoured the taste. 'What have they done to these? How can a vegetable taste like this?'

'They are good, aren't they?' Lucas looked much more at ease now he had told her why they were here. 'And yes. Apparently, he and my grandfather used to say we were destined for each other when we were babies and now he would like nothing better than that prophecy to come true.'

'And why is it such a problem? If you married her you wouldn't have to go around begging out-of-work actresses to pretend to be in love with you.'

'I don't want to marry *anyone* just yet. All my energies go into work, I don't have the emotional bandwidth for a wife and family now. And even if I did, well, Isabella has been raised in a very privileged way. She's never had to work a day in her life. Our values...' He shook his head. 'She's very beautiful but that's it. I don't need or want a trophy wife.'

'And how does she feel about you?'

'I don't know,' he said, looking uncomfortable now. 'She's very flirtatious, it's hard to know how serious she is, but Roberto takes her at face value. It's all very awkward. He's not well and I'm worried about him, which is why I'm going straight to his villa in Tuscany after I finish here tomorrow. But I just found out that not only is Isabella's latest engagement over but she will be staying there this week. I don't want her teasing to get his hopes up, not while he's unwell. He looked very frail last time I saw him...'

Some of Tally's amusement at the absurd situation she had found herself in ebbed away. This wasn't the slightly farcical, possibly sordid scenario his proposition had first conjured up but a man trying to do the right thing, although in a rather clumsy way.

It was almost a shame that the whole idea was

obviously impossible. She rather liked the idea of Roberto and was intrigued by the glamorous Isabella. Not to mention a week's stay in a Tuscan villa. But of course she couldn't say yes. It wasn't acting; it was deception.

Wasn't it?

'And there's no one else you could ask? No occasional date, no one whose DMs you've been sliding into, no amenable ex who can help you out?'

'Like I said, the business needs my full attention.'

'Ah, the elusive work-life balance. It's nice to see it in action.'

'So, what do you think?'

What she should think was this was the most absurd idea she had ever heard. But on the other hand, she had just played the most stereotypical parody of a French maid because she had lost out on the opportunity of a lifetime. What was waiting for her back in London apart from her childhood attic bedroom, shifts behind the bar, long anxious hours waiting to hear from her agent and crushing disappointment? She speared an asparagus and looked over at Lucas.

'It depends,' she said. 'Partly on how you think this will work and whatever the going rate is for a fake girlfriend these days and partly on how I feel about it. Can we drop it for now while I mull it over?'

'Of course.'

The rest of the meal was as delicious as the starters had promised, Lucas a sometimes amusing, if serious bordering on occasionally brooding companion but as the sky darkened, the stars replaced the sun and the lighting became more intimate, Tally was aware of a low feeling in her stomach, her chest, one that was almost disappointment. What had she expected this evening to be? Certainly not a job offer. For a moment there she had thought she might be enjoying a fairy tale moment, something not quite real, that wouldn't translate into the real world where their lives were so very different but a lovely memory, something to help restore her tattered self-esteem, to bury any vestiges of longing for Max and the life he had shattered.

But who was she kidding? Rich, successful businessmen didn't fall for jobbing actresses, not in the real world. Of *course* he was offering her a job. The attraction she had felt in the cabin, that shiver of awareness, the surprising pleasure she had felt at seeing him this morning were one-sided and that was to be expected. He wanted her professional skills only. It made complete sense and she was silly to take it so personally.

It was just… Her world was one of artifice, of characters played and discarded, of smiles and quips and occasional authority when she was behind the bar. When did she get a chance to be herself? Tallulah May Jenkins? She would have quite liked it to be Tallulah sitting here in this idyllic location with this gorgeous success-ful man on an actual date, not Tally, about to haggle over the terms of a contract.

If she accepted it, that was. And although it was just a job Lucas West was offering her, nothing more sordid, it still felt wrong. Lovely as a week in Tuscany and any number of un-specified black-tie events sounded, she was going to have to say no. And as she made the decision, she knew he sensed it, some of the in-timacy replaced by his usual formality. He was ever the courteous host but she could tell that he too was playing a part. That he often did. That maybe he was so used to it he had no idea where the mask ended and the real-life Lucas began.

It was intriguing, but none of her business. So best not to dwell on what was going on under that courteous expression—or wonder about what seemed to be a well-honed body under the expensive clothes. Best not to feel like she scored a point every time he reluctantly almost smiled or feel like she had scored a goal when he even more reluctantly laughed. It wasn't her job to get to know him. And whatever her answer, tonight was work.

Tally toyed with the remains of her risotto. It was amazing, as was the glass of red wine that accompanied it, but she couldn't appreciate either of them properly, aware that Lucas was awaiting her answer.

'I…' she began, just as he started to speak.

'Thank you…'

She stopped, a little relieved by the delay. 'You first.'

'No, I interrupted you. What were you going to say?'

'Just that I have had a lovely time tonight. Thank you so much for asking me and for making it possible with the flights and the room. I am really grateful…' She paused, searching for the right words.

But he was way ahead of her. 'But you're not comfortable accepting my proposal?'

'No.' Tally was grateful to Lucas for making it so easy. 'I understand your reasons, but…' she started, distracted by the sound of her phone. Who on earth was calling her? Even her grandmother preferred messaging, usually with a series of emojis that were harder to decipher than the most complicated cryptic crossword. 'I'm sorry, it's probably spam. Let me send it to voicemail.' She lifted her phone out of her bag and hesitated when she saw her friend Layla's name flashing on the screen. 'Hang on.'

She pressed accept. 'Layla? Is everything okay?' She smiled apologetically at Lucas, who nodded and turned his attention to the pudding menu the waiter had placed in front of them.

'Tal, I'm sorry, I know you're away with work. Is this a good time?'

Not a butt dial then. 'It's fine, I have a minute. What's going on?'

'It's the wedding.'

Tally froze. Layla wouldn't be calling unless it was a crisis. Her oldest friend was marrying her childhood sweetheart in just a few weeks' time and, as maid of honour, Tally had been involved in what felt like every detail, from helping Phinn plan the perfect proposal to researching honeymoon destinations. There had been Say Yes to the Dress moments, a hen night in Brighton, more hours than she could count sitting in Layla's sitting room making table decorations and place cards and helping reorganise the table plan for the thirtieth time. There was still an old-fashioned night-before-the-wedding hen night in the pub to enjoy—but not too much, as Layla wanted everyone tucked up by ten—and bridesmaid duties on the day itself. The whole event had been a welcome distraction from her still lingering heartsoreness over her own breakup and crushing disappointment workwise. She was almost as invested in the wedding as the bride and groom. She wasn't sure she could cope with a crisis.

'The wedding?'

'I swear I had no idea,' Layla continued.

'Idea about what? Layla, the wedding *is* still on, isn't it?' Increasingly lurid thoughts were passing through her mind. Phinn was the mildest man possible, a primary school teacher who liked nothing better than a gruelling walk through icy winds to some barren peak followed by a pint in a pub and a game of Scrabble, a startling contrast to life-and-soul city girl Layla, but somehow they worked. Had Phinn been cheating? Had Layla? She'd know, wouldn't she?

'Of course the wedding is still on, idiot. But annoyingly with the addition of your ex. I had no idea Phinn had actually invited him until I got a text today asking for a plus-one. Cheeky sod. Oh, I'm so cross with Phinn. He knew we got you in the breakup. Obviously.'

But it wasn't that simple, was it? For four years they had been a foursome. Tally and Max, Layla and Phinn, meals out, weekends away, long evenings in her mother's pub. They'd all been roped into Charlene's Christmas panto-mimes more than once and gone along to cheer her successful Shakespeare and a Pint summer initiative. If Tally and Max hadn't broken up then he would have been an integral part of this wedding, probably an usher. It wasn't fair to expect Phinn not to invite him. Or not to allow him a plus-one.

And Tally would have to smile and be gra-cious and not weep into her wine or flirt out-rageously with someone else or beg Max to take her back because it was Phinn and Layla's day—but, oh, God, it was going to be hard. She hadn't even seen him in months and now she was going to have to watch him dance with someone else, kiss someone else. Love someone else.

'Is it too late to turn my bridesmaid's dress into something really showstopping?' She tried to sound amused rather than devastated. 'I know technically it's your day but, under the circumstances, it seems the only option.'

'We'll take it up to mid-thigh and down to your navel if you forgive me.'

'Sounds great.' She looked over at Lucas, his gaze fixed on his phone. Summer events, he had said. Plus-one at weddings and business events. Surely that would go both ways? She wouldn't need a fabulous dress and a game face if she had someone like Lucas West on her arm. Checkmate, Max. Tally rapidly recalled the last incarnation of the seating plan she had seen. There was space. 'But what would be even more helpful is if I can have a plus-one too. I'll pay, of course.'

'Don't be ridiculous. I'm sure we can manage another chicken somehow. But a plus-one? *Who?*'

Layla's surprise wasn't unexpected but it was a little depressing. Surely Tally's prospects weren't *that* bad?

'I'll fill you in later. Tell Phinn I forgive him but if he ever hurts you...'

'You'll end him, I know.'

'As long as he knows. Thanks for the heads-up. I have to go. Love you.'

She finished the call, sat back and picked up her wine glass, needing Dutch courage. Was she actually going to do this?

'I accept,' she said. 'But not for money, not as a job, but as a reciprocal agreement. I have a wedding of my own I need to attend in a few weeks and my ex will be there with a plus-one.'

Understanding filled Lucas's gaze. 'I see.'

'Yes, well,' she said uncomfortably. 'It was almost a year ago and I should have moved on by now. I *have* moved on.' Kind of. 'But I am petty enough to want to show him that. So, here's what I propose. I will spend this week in Tuscany with you and in return you will come to Layla's wedding with me. No wages, we are doing each other a favour. If things go well and we both want to carry on then we discuss the rest of the summer after the wedding.'

Lucas's eyes narrowed assessingly as he thought her proposal through. 'Agreed.'

'If any other events come up between Tuscany and the wedding then I am happy to accompany you, but I'll need some notice. I'll have some shifts to do at the pub, hopefully some auditions.' Speaking of which, she needed to let her mother know she wouldn't be home for a week.

'Agreed,' he said again. 'But one caveat. I will supply you with a wardrobe for this week and for any other event you accompany me to.'

'There's no need for that,' she protested, although she knew her protest was unconvincing as she mentally assessed the smarter parts of her wardrobe and found them sadly wanting.

'There's every need,' he said grimly. 'Roberto is supposed to be resting but he may have organised parties, dinners out, opera trips. You need to be convincing as my girlfriend and that means looking the part. I'll get Candace to send you a list of possible occasions and dress codes and transfer you the funds you'll need. I have a few meetings tomorrow so you can have the day to shop. I'll meet you around three-thirty. It's a four-hour journey to Tuscany, so be prepared.'

'New wardrobe. Fed and watered. Got it.' She felt a little dizzy—it was all happening so fast.

'Good.' He paused, looking a little uncomfortable. 'And Tally, thank you.'

'No need to thank me. You are doing me just as big a favour. It's a reciprocal agreement.'

'A reciprocal agreement,' he echoed. 'Right.'

Tally took another sip of her wine. It wasn't hard to decipher the doubt in his tone. Lucas West was clearly someone who was used to paying for what he needed. His PA booked his restaurants, he would send his shirts out to be ironed, why not purchase a plus-one too? She'd shifted the whole arrangement. Made them equals. It would be fun seeing how he managed that.

* * *

Tally was waiting as arranged by the vaporetto stop. Punctuality was a good sign, Lucas thought as the boat's deckhand carried her bags onto the boat he had arranged to take them to the outskirts of the city where roads replaced canals and a car awaited. His gaze fell on the luggage piled up beside her. He'd directed that a prepaid credit card be delivered to the hotel that morning and, judging by the number of cases, Tally had made good use of it.

'I don't normally travel with so much stuff,' she said breathlessly as she climbed onto the small boat. 'That big case is actually my costumes—luckily, Neil doesn't need them back just yet. Those two bags are new. I bought a ridiculous amount for one week but you did say to be prepared for every eventuality and I took you at your word. Only this small one is actually mine.' She must have seen his gaze linger on the two new bags and added a little defensively, 'I've already sent all the receipts to your PA. It's harder work than you know shopping for a whole new wardrobe in just a few hours. I thought it would be like a movie montage, with me swirling around in huge skirts and looking cute in hats while assistants applauded but instead it was like a really messy supermarket sweep.'

'I'm sure whatever you got will be fine.' He took in her current outfit, a pink striped jumpsuit with a matching pink headband holding back her mass of wavy hair. 'Is that new?'

'It is. It kind of gave me fifties Riviera vibes. Too much?'

Lucas's mouth was unexpectedly dry. 'No,' he managed after an excruciatingly long moment. 'Not too much. You look…nice.' What she looked like was strawberry ice-cream, sweet and enticing with a hint of spice. The jumpsuit showed off her long legs to perfection, nipping in at her waist then flaring out with delicious ruffles across her chest. 'It's fine.'

To his relief, his phone lit up once they were underway and he spent the short ride to the car park in conversation with his lawyers, switching to hands-free once they were out of the city and he had the measure of the car he'd hired. Tally merely gave him an amused glance when one call immediately replaced the other, busying herself on her phone or looking out of the window but, despite himself, Lucas was always aware of her, of the swish of her hair, her floral scent, every shift and small sound.

The time passed quickly, the powerful car

eating up the miles, the calls occupying his mind as they drove south, and it wasn't until they entered the green hilly countryside of Tuscany that his phone finally stopped ringing.

Tally shifted to look at him. 'Okay,' she said. 'Time to concentrate on the mission. We need to establish our story arc.'

'Our *what*?'

'Our meet-cute, our history. What should we already know about each other? What stage are we at?'

Lucas blinked. This was already more complicated than he had envisioned. But then he hadn't really thought about what would happen after she had said yes, hadn't thought she *would* say yes or even that he would ask her at all. And this was why he didn't do impulsive.

'I thought we would tell the truth,' he said slowly. 'We met on the Orient Express and...'

What came next? They were attracted to each other? He couldn't deny that he *was* attracted to Tally but that was a complication he had no intention of adding to what was already a stressful situation.

'I invited you along,' he finished, aware it wasn't the most compelling story. 'Keep it as simple as we can.'

'Hmm...' Tally tapped her fingers on her knee

as she considered. 'It would do if you were simply inviting me to a party, but not for a week away. It's a bit much to ask someone you've known for two days to someone else's house and, more importantly, it's not going to be the deterrent you need.'

'Okay then, what do you suggest?'

'Where do you live?'

'London.'

'Whereabouts in London?' she said patiently.

'Chelsea. My father had a house there and I use that,' he added, aware that she was right, she needed some personal details. 'My mother still lives in the family's Yorkshire estate when she's in the UK. I spend some time there but mostly I'm in London or here in Italy or travelling.'

'You don't sound like a Yorkshireman. Okay, Chelsea is perfect.'

'Is it?'

'Absolutely. My stepfather's pub is off the King's Road. You might even have been in it. In fact, for this story you *have* been in it. Let me think…' The tapping intensified but for once Lucas didn't mind the distracting noise. 'Right, you came in for a pint a few months ago—is that something you would do?'

'Maybe. Occasionally.'

'All we need is occasional.' She tapped some more, her eyes fixed unseeingly on the horizon. 'I was behind the bar; it was a quiet night and we flirted a bit.'

If Lucas had been wearing a tie he would have loosened it. He tried to imagine himself walking into a pub and casually flirting with a pretty barmaid. With *this* pretty barmaid. 'Right,' he managed.

'After that we saw each other a few times around, the way you do when you're aware of someone and they seem to be everywhere. You know?'

Just like bumping into Tally in that mask shop. Had that really been just yesterday morning?

'Then we ended up having a drink together. But I was still raw over Max and you were busy and things kind of tailed off...'

'That sounds a bit weak,' he objected. 'How about I was called away on a secret mission or you got amnesia?'

She laughed. 'Unexpectedly vivid imagination. I like it, but as your friends are unlikely to believe the secret mission and mine know I didn't have amnesia let's go with you being really busy and then I had a big audition I needed to concentrate on and so we didn't break up

exactly, we weren't really together, but it came
to an end. However, we've both been thinking
about reaching out and so yay, what a fabulous coincidence to bump into each other on
the train and here we are.'

Lucas thought about it, testing her story as if
it were a new product, idea, brand, stretching
and examining, looking for holes and weaknesses. It wasn't the most dramatic origin story
but it had the ring of truth and that was probably more important than high drama or romance. 'Agreed.'

'So, what did we talk about on those walks
and almost dates? Let me see. Tally Jenkins,
sometime actress, more time barmaid, you
know that. I grew up over the pub with my mum
and stepdad, Steve. They got married when I
was five and Steve is my dad to all intents and
purposes.'

'Do you ever see your real father?'

'No. I've never seen him, never heard from
him. Child maintenance was paid monthly
until the month I left school and then stopped.
It couldn't be clearer that he wants nothing to
do with me.' She said the words almost air-
ily, with the ease of long practice, but Lucas
couldn't help thinking that she said them as if
by saying it they were true. He got that. He was

president of the club for growing up with disappointing self-interested fathers after all. 'Okay, my best friend is Layla, who is a teacher, and marrying Phinn, another teacher. You are coming to their wedding with me. I was with Max for four years. I think that's everything vital.'

'Why did you break up?'

'Different values, the usual.' She bit her lip. 'When I met Max he was in a band, the day job in finance was just to pay the bills, but at some point that changed. The band became first a hobby and was then replaced by cycling and the job became a career and he was ready for a mortgage, settling down, kids. A girlfriend with an uncertain income who is sometimes around all the time or might be away for a week or weeks or even months doesn't fit with that lifestyle. In the end he said it was the job or him.'

'And you chose the job?'

She looked away. 'I said I didn't do ultimatums. So, I am back living above the pub, auditioning and doing my best to prove him wrong in every way and succeeding badly.'

'Which is why you need a plus-one?'

'Exactly. Okay, what will I need to know about you to pass the still fairly new girlfriend test? Name? Star sign? Favourite pet?'

'You know my name.'

'You don't have a middle name?'

'I don't think that's relevant.'

Lucas concentrated on the road ahead but was aware of Tally twisting around in her seat to stare at him, a grin lighting up her face.

'You *do* have a middle name! And one you hate at that. Hmm, let me see. Cedric? St John? Lancelot?'

'I sincerely hope you are never the mother of sons.'

'I'm just guessing, not suggesting them for our future imaginary offspring. Come on,' she coaxed. 'How bad can it be?'

'It's not *bad*,' he said a little stiffly. 'It's just embarrassing.'

'Come on, Lucas, isn't this exactly the kind of thing you'd confide on a springtime walk in the park?'

'No, it's the kind of thing that makes me want to change my name by deed poll. Okay—' as she started to speak again '—it's Jupiter. Okay?'

Tally didn't answer and when he glanced over, he saw her gazing at him in fascination. *'No,'* she half whispered at last. 'Really? As in king of the gods. Wow. That's a lot to live up to.'

'You can see why I don't advertise the fact.'

'It could have been worse,' she said after a while. 'It could have been Mars. Or Hades, although Pluto is the Roman variant, isn't it? Not that Pluto is any better.'

'My mother was a classicist. She wanted Jupiter to be my first name but my father for once did the sensible thing and said no. They compromised on a middle name.'

'You have a brother, don't you?'

'Yes, Felix.'

'Please tell me he's been saddled with Hercules or Apollo.'

Despite himself, Lucas couldn't help a half smile. 'Neptune.'

'Wow. Any sisters, a lucky Proserpina or Venus? Although you could get away with a Diana or Minerva quite easily, I suppose.'

'No sisters. Just two sons with slightly out-there middle names even by *The Times* birth column standards. Otherwise, we had a pretty normal certain class of English upbringing. Home between Yorkshire and London, prep school at seven then Eton. A bored and angry mother who drank too much, spent too much, had too many affairs and a spendthrift, negligent father whose claim to fame was being on the front page of the tabloids kissing the inner thigh of a cabinet minister's wife. That,' he added grimly, 'was a fun day at school. No pets as we were never in one place long enough. My birthday is October, whatever that means star sign wise. I left school at eighteen as you know and took over the business when my father died, mother alive but lives in the Bahamas and occasionally plays lady of the manor in Yorkshire. We're not close. I *am* close to Felix. No significant relationships; I have been concentrating on work and that seems to be an issue after a few months for most women, hence the need for you.'

He didn't have to look at Tally to know she would be open-mouthed and wide-eyed. He wasn't sure what had led him to say all that, especially the part about his father. It was no secret, google Peter West and it was still the most significant part of his Wiki bio, but it wasn't information he usually freely volunteered. Nor did he usually show his bitterness and anger quite so clearly.

'Okay,' Tally said after a while. 'I think you know most of the pertinent things about me. Single mum, pub, stepdad, reluctant and yet still going actress, recent heartbreak. I grew up with a selection of pub cats, most beloved was the very originally named Tabby, who lived to eighteen and was still coaxing titbits until the day she died. Never had a dog, always wanted one.'

'Me too,' he volunteered, surprised at himself. He'd long forgotten that old yearning for a dog.

'There you go, the thing we have in common.'

'Star sign, Aquarius…' Of course she knew that. 'No siblings. The only thing you don't know that you should is about my father. He's kind of…oh!' As he turned off the road into the gates leading into Roberto's villa and vineyard, 'Is this it? Oh, my goodness, I wasn't expecting this! This gig gets better by the day!'

CHAPTER FIVE

TALLY HADN'T KNOWN what to expect from her residence for the next week; Tuscan villa as a concept was somewhat outside her experience, but whatever she had imagined, it certainly wasn't as grand and yet welcoming as the vista that greeted them. Arched, elegantly designed iron gates ushered them into a sweeping drive, rows of vines all around, stretching out as far as the eye could see, undulating green hills in the background. The drive had been long and now it was late evening, the sun was low on the horizon, casting a warm golden glow over the idyllic scene.

In the distance she could see a pink building and as they got closer exclaimed in delight as she took in balustraded balconies, a sweet little turret on one corner, an entire tower complete with narrow windows perfect for shooting arrows out of on the other side. Formal gardens were laid out in front of the villa arranged across shallow terraces, while orange, lemon and olive trees clustered together in an orchard on the far side.

'Wow…' she breathed again, her vocabulary deserting her. 'This is really something. How old is it?'

'Part of the villa dates back hundreds of years. Roberto's family has made wine here for generations on his mother's side. His father's family are from Milan.'

'Hence the business connection, I suppose. I like clothes well enough—' she couldn't help smoothing down the linen jumpsuit as she spoke, feeling slightly guilty as she remembered just how much of a spree she had gone on, panicking at all the unknowns that lay before her as she bought enough clothes for a month not a week '—but overall, I am team wine, especially if it's produced somewhere as beautiful as this.'

'You and Roberto both. He spent most of his life in Milan, expanded the family business diligently, but his heart was always here. He has passed the clothing side onto his son, but nothing would prise him away from his vines. Not even doctor's orders.'

A momentary cloud passed over Lucas's face. It was hard to get a reading on her make-believe boyfriend most of the time, but one thing Tally did know: he really did love Roberto. She liked that about him, the way he so willingly attributed his success to the mentorship of another. He might be proud but he wasn't prideful.

He pulled the car into a small car park towards the back of the house, a dusty square surrounded by low buildings that looked as if they had once been stables. 'Okay, ready?'

Tally took a deep breath. 'Almost. There's one thing we haven't established.'

His brow creased. 'What's that? I have family, pets and exes memorised. Do I need your favourite colour as well?'

'It varies depending on mood. Today it's pink, as you can see. But no, nothing so simple. What we need to do is establish how we are when we are together.'

Establishing trust when playing lovers or a love scene was usually a slow process, built up layer by layer. A light touch, eye contact, a slow dance to intimacy, usually directed by someone else. But there was no time for any of that. In a couple of minutes' time Tally was going to have to convince two strangers that she and Lucas were reunited lovers, still in the honeymoon stage, so attached they couldn't bear to be parted now they had found each other once again.

More importantly, Lucas was going to have to do the same, only his role was much harder. These people knew him, could read him, were aware of his business first, love last approach to life. They were bound to be sceptical, unsure of Tally, and their current body language wouldn't fool anyone, especially not someone who knew Lucas intimately.

'We need to act like we're in love,' she clarified.

'Right.' His expression, as usual, gave nothing away but she thought she saw a flicker of alarm in his eyes. 'Well, we've got our stories straight so...'

'So that's part one, but it's no good *telling* people we're mad about each other, we have to *show* them. We have to be consistent, believable with every look and tone and movement.' She unbuckled her seatbelt and turned to face him. 'Look at me.'

Slowly, Lucas shifted until he was mirroring her, his shoulders as set as his actually rather marvellous mouth.

'Look at me again,' she said, her voice low, intent. One casting director had described that particular tone as like molten honey. 'Look at me as if I'm the only person you want to see, as if everyone else and everything else is merely a distraction, as if you're just waiting until you can get me alone and...'

Her mouth dried up, her imagination not failing her but instead supplying her with a dizzying array of images detailing exactly what Lucas might do to her and she to him when alone. She could feel her breath hitch, her neck and chest flush, heat pool low in her stomach before spreading out and down, an ache sweet and painful between her legs. She allowed her gaze to linger on the hard lines of his mouth, tracing every millimetre of his lips, to dip down, past his stubbled chin to the exposed vee of his throat then back up, up, up until she met his gaze, his eyes darkened to a fierce navy like a storm-tossed sea. He no longer seemed guarded but nor was he vulnerable. Instead, he was looking at her as if he could see through her, right to the heart of her, as if the pink and white jumpsuit didn't exist. The ache intensified and her lips parted, her body swaying towards his, her hand reaching up as if by its own volition to touch his cheek.

'Lucas,' she breathed, only to jump back, the spell shattered, as a hand rapped on the window. He drew back, his gaze still fixed on hers, a pulse beating in his cheek.

'Lesson learned,' she said shakily, trying to

recover her equilibrium. 'Good job. Just try to channel that every now and then and we should be fine.'

It had happened before, she told herself as she fumbled with the door handle, this crossing of lines from faking to feeling. It happened all the time. That was why sets and rehearsal rooms were rife with flings and affairs. Acting wasn't pretending, it was being, and if she was to do her job well, she had to let herself fall into the illusion. It was just a good thing Lucas was an apt pupil.

But as she slid out of the car and found herself enthusiastically greeted by a clearly unwell Roberto, who refused the stick his assistant tried to give him and could only be dissuaded from taking her bag by Lucas taking his arm and walking him firmly back to the house, she couldn't help wondering just how much acting she had been doing in the end. She had to be careful. She was here to do a job, paid or not. It wasn't real, no matter how swept up in the moment she had been.

The late evening sun was real though, the air, sweet and fragrant with herbs and citrus and summer flowers was real, the gorgeous old villa was real, cool and shady inside, with high ceilings and tiled floors. Lucas had disappeared with Roberto—so much for proving to everyone that they couldn't keep their hands off each other.

But, on the other hand, even without knowing Roberto she could see his skin was sallow, his hands shaky, that there was an air of frailty around him, one he seemed to want to deny. She could also see how worried Lucas was, saw the care with which he escorted the older man. It was a good sign, showed she hadn't been misled by him, that there was a good heart under the remote manner and tailored suits.

Elena, Roberto's assistant, still carrying the rejected stick, suggested that she might want time to freshen up before dinner and, after four hours in the car, Tally agreed. She was led through the large welcoming entrance hall, down a wide tiled corridor and up a winding staircase to a pretty sitting room, its half-shuttered windows overlooking the vineyard. A second staircase in the corner led up to a semi-circular bedroom with two doors on one side. Tally took in the curved walls on one side, set with three charmingly leaded windows, each with a cosy window seat set beneath them, and realised with delight that her room was in the turret she had admired from the car. The whole was painted white with the wooden floor polished to a warm golden glow. The room was large, a huge bed dominating the middle, two inviting-looking chairs either side of a low table against the opposite wall. A huge olive rug lay on the floor, the same colour picked up in the blinds, cushions and bedlinen, abstract nature inspired prints on the walls.

'Oh, this is gorgeous,' she exclaimed.

'Your bathroom is through here,' Elena explained, opening one of the doors in the wall bisecting the room. 'Can I bring you anything? Wine, coffee?'

Both sounded amazing but Tally wasn't even used to room service in hotels—she counted it an upgrade if there was a coffee machine instead of plastic sachets—so she shook her head diffidently. 'Oh, no, but thank you.'

'Drinks are being served on the terrace; dinner will be in about thirty minutes. Can you find your way back downstairs?'

Two staircases, a corridor, another staircase. Maybe.

'I'm sure I'll be fine,' she said, not sure at all. 'Thank you again.'

'*Prego.*'

Elena nodded and headed back down the stairs, leaving Tally to continue looking around. They had headed straight here but somehow her cases had preceded her and had been set next to the bathroom door. The bathroom contained an inviting-looking standalone tub alongside a rainfall shower so big it was practically a wet room with two sinks lined up under the mirror. Another door led to the loo, discreetly hidden away in its own little room with another sink. The double doors next to the bathroom led, not into a walk-in closet as she had imagined, but into an entire dressing area with open built-in wardrobes and a dressing table.

'Wow…' she murmured again, grabbing her phone and taking a picture to send to Layla. 'I don't want to ever leave. Look at this.'

Tally grabbed her cases and dragged them into the dressing room, quickly hanging up a few dresses and tops she thought might crease, leaving the rest to be dealt with later. She unpacked her make-up bag and wash bag, leaving the first on the dressing table, carrying the second through to the bathroom, where she washed her hands and face, before quickly reapplying some concealer, mascara and lipstick and combing her hair.

She would have to do. Anything more and she would be late for dinner.

Cautiously, Tally made her way down the winding staircase to the sitting room below. It was all part of the same suite, she realised, decorated in the same olive and crisp white tones, with two comfortable sofas, a bookcase filled with books in Italian and English and a thick rug softening the stone floor. At one end she spied a small kitchenette containing a kettle and toaster. Thank goodness she would be able to fend for herself after all. No awkward summoning of staff for a cup of tea. Whatever the rest of the week would bring, she had been housed very well. First the Orient Express, then her very comfortable if slightly anonymous hotel room and now all this spacious splendour. The two rooms together were bigger than her and Max's flat, let alone her bedroom above the pub.

Speaking of Max. She had to soft launch Lucas in a believable way. Max might have blocked her but most of his friends hadn't. She checked the time and then quickly took a selfie, leaning against a window, the setting sun behind her. She posted it, adding a few hashtags—#nofilter #tuscany #vineyard #unexpectedbreak—and captioned the whole Begin Again, selecting the Taylor Swift song of the same name to accompany it.

Ha. Max had never liked her to wear high heels either, she thought as the lyrics ran through her mind, but at over six foot she doubted Lucas would have similar hangups. Most people exchanged their bridesmaid's shoes for something more comfortable for the evening part of a wedding but Tally vowed that she was going to exchange hers for the most vertiginous heels she owned.

Picture posted, she slipped her phone back into her pocket and set about trying to retrace her steps. Forget Rapunzel, this felt like Hansel and Gretel. If only she had thought to sprinkle some breadcrumbs on her hurried journey to her room.

Lucas checked his watch. 'Maybe I should go check on Tally…' he began when, right on cue, she rushed onto the terrace, breathless with apology.

'I'm not late, am I?' she asked anxiously. 'I assured the nice lady who showed me to my room that I would easily find my way back but I got hopelessly lost. You have a lovely home,' she added. 'I know this now because I have explored every inch.'

Roberto laughed and took Tally's hands in his. 'I am glad you approve. Now, what can I get you? Prosecco? A Pinot Grigio grown here on the estate, or something a little richer?'

'Prosecco would be lovely, but only if there is one open. Do you make that here as well?'

'I don't grow the Glera grapes needed, but it is local and organic.' Roberto handed her a glass. 'And how do you like your room?'

'Oh, it's amazing. I feel like a princess in there, real Rapunzel vibes, thank you.'

As he watched Tally charm Roberto, Lucas felt his worries unfurl. He had made a good choice. She was seemingly totally natural and at ease.

'Isabella is out with friends but she should join us after dinner,' Roberto said as he led them towards a table in the corner of the terrace. 'So tonight, we dine al fresco, just an informal dinner amongst friends.'

Dinner was delicious, a simple but perfectly dressed salad before a small serving of rich and delicious pasta *arrabiata*, followed by chicken for Lucas and Roberto and fish for Tally. They ate slowly, Roberto and Tally discovering a mutual love of books and theatre and, to Lucas's relief, the conversation flowed naturally without much input from him.

He didn't mean to be so silent, to leave Tally to do the heavy lifting, but as the two chatted easily, recommending books and plays and films, he realised how much of his life, his conversation, his thoughts revolved around work. The books on his bedside table were about business, or histories of commerce and clothing, he listened to business podcasts when running or working out, rarely watched television and theatre was something he did to entertain or be entertained, along with the races and watching rugby and other forms of corporate hospitality. When had he last read for pleasure? When had he last done *anything* purely for pleasure?

His gaze fell on Tally, glowing in the candles and fairy lights as she gesticulated, so full of life and vibrancy it almost hurt, and his cheek tingled where she had touched it earlier, his whole body heating at the memory of her intense stare, the way she had leaned in, the scent of her. That was work for both of them, but there had been a painful pleasure there too.

The plates had been removed and a platter of fruit and cheese brought out to groans from Tally, who was proclaiming that this was one of the best meals she had ever eaten to protests from Roberto that it was nothing and he would remedy the simplicity this week, when a figure entered dramatically from the house, framed in the light spilling from the hallway. Tally might be an actress but Isabella instinctively knew how to stage a scene to her advantage. Roberto's granddaughter wore an off-the-shoulder tight-fitting black dress that hugged her slender curves, her hair sleek, framing her heart-shaped face. Large dark eyes regarded Lucas reproachfully.

'But Lucas, no one told me you were coming,' she said in Italian, ignoring Tally completely.

'Now, Isabella, I am sure I mentioned it yesterday. And English please, our other guest does not speak Italian,' Roberto remonstrated. 'Tally, this is Isabella, my granddaughter. Bella, meet Tally, Lucas's friend.'

Tally stood and held her hand out. 'So lovely to meet you. What a beautiful home you and your grandfather have here.'

Isabella's eyes flickered between Tally and Lucas before she took Tally's hand, like a queen bestowing a great favour on a lowly subject, and Lucas saw Tally's mouth twitch with amusement.

'Thank you. I spend most of my time in Rome or Paris, but it is nice to be in the country sometimes.' She dropped Tally's hand and into a seat in one languid movement. 'So, how long have you known each other? Luca, I thought you were too busy for *friends*.' She imbued the last word with meaning.

Lucas was more than grateful for Tally's foresight and professional skills as she expertly took Roberto and Isabella through the tale she had concocted with just the right amount of smiles across to Lucas, appeals to him to concur and one outstretched hand, which he took and squeezed, her skin silk under his touch.

Roberto listened with a benevolent smile, Isabella with narrow-eyed precision, questioning Tally closely, getting sulkier and sulkier as the story developed. Lucas knew that it wasn't, and had never been, that Isabella wanted him particularly. He had no title, he was rich, true, but everyone she knew was rich. No, it was more that Isabella was used to being worshipped by all who knew her and it irritated her that Lucas had never shown any inclination to join her court.

'You did brilliantly,' he said low-voiced as they stood after dinner, enjoying the warm evening air. Isabella had flounced off, clearly put out at not being the centre of attention, while Roberto was talking to the housekeeper as the table was cleared.

It wouldn't do for Lucas, living so closely and intimately with staff. The villa had three full-time members of staff, plus Roberto's long-standing assistant who accompanied him everywhere. His own assistant had never been to his flat, and he could see no reason why she would. His cleaning was done by an agency, he catered for himself or ate out. Even the Yorkshire estate, large as it was, had live-out cleaners and grounds people rather than live-in. But there was something comforting about seeing familiar faces, being greeted warmly, having the same room every time he came here. The villa was home in a way neither of his family houses were.

A thought belatedly occurred to him. 'Where are you staying?' he asked. Tally had said something about feeling like a princess and Lucas had a sinking feeling he knew exactly what that meant. And of course it did. This was the twenty-first century. It would be seen as odd not to put a couple, however short their relationship, into the same room.

'The turret, can you believe it? It's just incredible, the views and so beautiful. And of *course* you have seen it.' One of the things he liked about Tally was how quick she was on the uptake. 'It's *your* room, isn't it? That makes sense. I can't believe we didn't discuss the whole sleeping arrangement part.'

'The sofas in the turret sitting room are very comfortable,' he said hurriedly.

'I'll take them. I can't turn you out of your bed. I'll just say your snoring drove me away.'

Her smile was low and intimate and stirred something deep inside him. It was hard not to imagine her in his bed, a mass of chestnut hair spread over the pillow, the sheet revealing more than it concealed, that particular wicked smile curving her full lips and... *Good God*, he needed a cold shower. And how was he supposed to get any sleep with that image in his head?

'No, you're my guest. I'll take the sofa,' he said brusquely. 'Can you find your own way there? I want to make sure Roberto gets to his room okay.'

Tally glanced over at their host. 'He's been on really good form all evening, but he does look tired now. I hope I didn't overdo it.'

'No, no, I think he's had a lovely evening, the two of you had so much to talk about...' He hesitated, not sure whether the lively conversation had been part of her persona. That, in some way, would feel worse than pretending they were together. To let Roberto feel he had found a kindred spirit but all along it was fake, but to his relief she nodded in agreement.

'He's such a theatre buff. Some of the things he has seen are, like, totally legendary. I'm in awe.'

'In awe of what?'

He hadn't heard Roberto walk up behind

them and he turned, glad the conversation was so innocuous. This double life was exhausting. He didn't mind a certain subterfuge in business, it was par for the course, but his personal life had always been straightforward. After untangling the mess of his father's affairs and dealing with the fallout of his mother's emotional messes, the last thing Lucas had ever wanted was a complicated love life of his own, real or fictional.

'Your life,' Tally said with a warm smile. 'You should write a book; I don't suppose you kept a diary? The things and people you have seen, I'd read it.'

'Sadly not, and even if I did, I am not sure it would be much use. Probably a detailed account of what I ate, a briefer account of my day at work and, as a footnote, *I saw Laurence Olivier as Mark Antony. Not bad.*'

They all laughed but Lucas eyed Roberto with some concern. He was sallow rather than his usual olive, his eyes tired. Losing his father had been one thing, losing Roberto would be quite another.

'Let me walk you to your room,' he said, taking Roberto's arm.

'No, no, I can't allow you to neglect your lovely companion.'

'Not at all,' Tally said, dropping a kiss on Roberto's cheek as if she had known him for ever. 'It means I can get to the bathroom first, he's a terrible shower-hogger.' She winked at them and walked away, leaving both men looking after her appreciatively.

'I like her, Lucas.' As one they turned and walked slowly back into the villa, the older man leaning on the younger man's arm. 'She is fun, which you need, always so serious, but intelligent too, witty. I know I made no secret of my hopes for you and my Bella, the dreams of a foolish old man, but Bella needs an attentive man and you need a woman who will stop you brooding and working too hard. I like this Tally. I like her for you.'

'It's early days,' Lucas said, a little uncomfortable. One evening in and his plan was going better than he had expected but he didn't want Roberto to get too invested in Tally, not when she would be gone at the end of the summer, if not before. And if Roberto had already realised that Isabella and Lucas were not right for each other, had he needed to bring Tally along at all? By trying to do the right thing, had he just made everything far more complicated?

It was only one week. How invested could Roberto really get? But as his mind replayed the memory of Tally leaning towards him in the car, his cheek heating where she had touched him, he realised that maybe it wasn't Roberto he needed to worry about. If he wasn't careful, Lucas might be in danger too.

CHAPTER SIX

TALLY WOKE UP feeling as if she hadn't slept at all. It wasn't the fault of the bed, which was comfortable to a fault. The sun had risen early but the blinds did a good job of keeping the room cool and dark, and although they had eaten late, she had trained her digestion to manage that, used to post theatre meals and late suppers after evening pub shifts.

But her sleep had been fitful, her dreams vivid, full of trains and fear and intense blue eyes, dreams of weddings and standing in front of Max in a gold foil eighties-style bridesmaid's dress, while Isabella pouted on his arm and Lucas ignored her on the other side of the room. But worse had been the moments when she'd lain there awake, reliving the moment Lucas slipped out of the bathroom. Her light was off and she had pretended, for both their sakes, to be asleep. It felt a lot less awkward. But she had still been aware every moment he was in there, had heard the sound of the shower and had to work very hard not to imagine him under it. Had to work even harder not to relive the moment he left the bathroom, towel around a narrow waist, dark hair slicked back. She had been right, there was a very fine body under those suits, lean and muscled in all the right places, strong and capable…

Maybe this was a good thing. She was supposed to be attracted to him after all. Actually *being* attracted could only enhance her performance. And she hadn't fancied anyone since Max. This buzzing in her skin, heaviness in her belly, was a sign she was ready to get back out there.

She just needed to get through the next few weeks maintaining professional boundaries whilst playing the exact opposite. No big deal.

She hadn't heard Lucas get up, nor heard him come upstairs to use the bathroom, but when she got downstairs, showered and ready for the day in crisp red linen shorts paired with a sleeveless buttoned-up white shirt decorated with a red and blue nautical pattern, a red scarf taming her unruly waves and her sunglasses in her hand, she could see that he was long up and gone, the sheets from the sofa tidied away as if they had never been, his suitcases neatly to one side. One thing she needed to do was make it look a little more like they were cohabiting. But not until after coffee.

Breakfast was set up on the terrace where they had eaten last night. Lucas was already there, tapping away intently on his laptop, a slight frown pinching his forehead. Tally realised that she could probably count on one hand the number of times she had seen him smile, which was a shame, he was quite devastating when he did. Although he wasn't exactly unattractive now, shirt sleeves rolled up to show those really very capable-looking wrists, his nice tanned forearms, his equally capable fingers typing precisely, easily, not too fast and not too slow, and really, Tally, what on *earth* was she doing getting turned on by a man typing?

That was it, the final straw. Her libido was back and as soon as she had shown off her very handsome successful new beau to Max, she was going out and finding the perfect post-relationship relationship. Nothing too serious, something frivolous, a treat. Although it was a shame in some ways to squander the opportunity she had right here. Lucas wasn't frivolous, he was usually serious, but he was *definitely* a treat. He looked up and she half jumped, sure he could read her very inappropriate mind.

'Are you going to stand there and stare or are you going to join me?'

The table was set with a cheerful red cloth and held a basket of fresh-looking bread, a dish of olive oil, a selection of cheeses and hams, honeys and jams as well as delicious plates of fruit and a bowl of yogurt.

'I didn't want to disturb you, you looked so busy. Are you ever not working?' she added as she pulled a chair out and collapsed into it.

'Not really. Coffee?' She nodded and he poured some steaming coffee from a jug and passed it to her, followed by a milk jug. 'There's a lot to do.'

'But you must have other people who can take on some of the load. What about your brother?'

'Felix is a people person. He's invaluable for schmoozing, PR, that kind of thing. Really, it should have been him on the Orient Express not me, but he had been ill, which was why I stepped in.'

'Lucky for me,' she murmured, not really intending to be overheard, but he nodded.

'Lucky for both of us.'

'Although—' she lowered her voice although she couldn't see anyone within hearing distance '—Isabella certainly wasn't pleased to see me, I didn't get any hands-off-my-man vibes. I reckon you're safe from that direction at least.'

'Isabella was never the real issue, I knew I could handle her, it was more about not upsetting Roberto, but from something he said last night, I get the impression he knows that his dreams for Isabella and me are just that, that we wouldn't really suit. I think I have you to thank for that. He liked you a lot.'

'Me?' Tally felt absurdly touched. She had really enjoyed her conversation with their host the night before, it was nice to know the feeling was mutual. 'I doubt it. It was one evening, he barely knows me.'

'Ah, but he has always claimed to have good instincts.'

'Why, Mr West, are you complimenting me?'

His expression didn't change but his eyes were warm, and Tally grabbed her coffee, flustered.

Lucas returned his attention to his laptop while Tally concentrated on the excellent coffee and contemplated the array of food, quickly scrolling through her emails and messages as she did so. There was nothing in her email folder apart from offers for clothes she couldn't afford, restaurants she used to go to with Max and holidays she could only dream about. Nothing from her agent. She was used to the pang of disappointment, had lived with it for eight years, but it never seemed to lessen somehow. Indeed, since losing out on her last role it seemed worse somehow, as if her last chance had slipped by without her noticing it.

The group chats on the other side were predictably busy. She had messages in the hen night chat, the bridesmaids' chat, the one set up with her drama school friends, the never dull pub regulars' stream of nonsense, but she scrolled through them quickly, simply replying with a heart or other appropriate emoji.

Her mother had taken her decision to stay in Italy for a week with a surprising lack of questions, but Tally suspected Charlene was sick of her daughter moping around the flat and that she and Steve were glad of a few days' privacy. For people who had been married for twenty-five years, they could be horribly prone to PDAs. In fact, now she came to think of it, far more so than she and Max had ever been, even in the privacy of their own home.

Her reverie was broken by Roberto, who walked out apologising for his lateness and hoping they had all they needed. Even Lucas pushed his laptop away long enough to assure

Roberto that they were fine and the last thing he needed to do was worry.

'I was hoping to show you this beautiful region,' Roberto told Tally as he slowly lowered himself into a seat, Elena hovering behind him, clearly wanting to help but aware he would wave her off, irritated. 'But I find I am a little fatigued today.'

Lucas was instantly alert. 'You stayed up too late last night,' he scolded. 'Is having us here too much? We can go and stay elsewhere...'

'Not at all.' Roberto laid a hand on his arm. 'I am very glad you are here and that I get to spend time with Tally, but today I listen to my doctor and rest.' He pulled a face that made it clear how little he liked that idea. 'But you two must go out and explore.'

Tally didn't need to be a mind-reader to decipher Lucas's expression. 'Lucas has work to do, but I can entertain myself very well. I'm sure there are lovely walks around here.'

'You can borrow my car,' Lucas said, clearly relieved, but Tally shook her head.

'I don't drive. Born and bred Londoner. There's a bus every five minutes. But I'm very self-sufficient, promise. I'll be fine.' A vineyard, beautiful scenery, a tempting-looking pool. She was sure she would manage.

'Absolutely not,' Roberto said. 'Lucas can take a day off every now and then. Maybe even two. Visit Siena, Lucca, San Gimignano. Go on a wine-tasting tour or two, I can arrange that for you, and then when I have more energy we will go to Florence and I will take you to my favourite restaurant. What do you think?'

'It all sounds *amazing*,' Tally said, trying not to sound too eager and put Lucas on the spot. 'But honestly, I was an unexpected last-minute guest and no one needs to put themselves out for me.'

Her arguments were fruitless. Roberto had it all planned out and unless they wanted to upset an elderly man, they had no choice but to agree.

'I meant it, you really don't have to worry about me,' she said to Lucas as they walked back to their turret. 'Just drop me off somewhere and you can come back here while I explore. I don't mind.'

'And upset Roberto? Impossible. Besides, he was right. Maybe I *can* take a day off.'

Tally stopped and whirled around to face him. 'You can what? Do you want to say that again for the camera?' She pulled out her phone and held it teasingly up as if recording, laughing at his exasperated expression.

'It's not that big a deal, I do take time off occasionally,' he said, but she could have sworn his mouth was twitching with a rare smile.

'Well, I'm honoured one of these rare times is with me. Okay, let me get a few things together. I'll meet you back down here.'

She skipped off to her room trying to quell the excitement in her stomach. It was just a day sightseeing, not a declaration. But Tally couldn't help feeling that workaholic Lucas willingly choosing to spend time with her over work was a very good sign indeed.

Tally's *few things* included a bag with a change of shoes, a cardigan and scarf, two different types of suntan lotion, water bottles, a hat and some snacks as well as a battery pack and a book. Lucas had changed into shorts and a short-sleeved shirt and was ready long before she was but, to his surprise, he wasn't irritated by her absent-minded packing and her several rememberings of *just one more thing* before they were finally on their way.

Nor did he mind the loss of a day as much as he'd thought he would. How could he when the sun shone, the landscape was idyllic and his companion clearly ready to enjoy the experience? Besides, he didn't need to lose the whole day. There would be plenty of places he could work while Tally went sightseeing.

'I've always wanted to visit Italy,' she confided as he drove round sweeping curves, the hills and vineyards unfolding in front of them. 'I can't believe I'm here at last.'

'All of Italy or any particular part?'

'All of it from Sicily to the Dolomites. I think it's always felt like the ultimate in sophistication, you know, all those Regency youths on their grand tours and Edwardians in Florence.'

'Why didn't you visit before?'

'That's a very good question. We didn't really do holidays when I was young. We were too poor before Mum married Steve and then afterwards there was the pub. He didn't like leaving it, especially in school holidays because they were the busiest times. Now I can usually take over so they can get away, but back then we were lucky to get a weekend in Margate and that was before the hipsters moved in. Layla and I went on a couple of holidays, but that was more *"lads, lads, lads"*, you know? Cheap, and as cheerful as too many shots could make it and devoid of any culture whatsoever.' She laughed. 'Fun, though.'

'And what about with your ex? Max, isn't

it?' He could feel his jaw tighten just saying his name.

Tally bit her lip. 'Max is very outdoorsy. His idea of a perfect holiday is carrying all your clothes on your back and walking from one remote spot to another or taking a very small boat onto a very large body of water or dangling off a cliff face on a rope, those kinds of things. And he had a lot more money than me, so he tended to go away with his friends.'

'You never holidayed together?' Lucas wasn't sure why he sounded so horrified. After all, he'd never been the romantic holiday type himself.

'Oh, we did, but not the kind of exploring culture with added sunshine holidays I wanted, more short breaks or holidays where he could do his thing. A house by the sea with friends, a hotel in the Lake District, that sort of thing. It was nice, but very much on his terms. Plus...' She shifted, and when he glanced over at her, he could see that she was gazing out of the window, her oversized sunglasses shielding her expression.

'Plus what?'

'Oh, it was just another battle in the war of our relationship. That I couldn't just take time off like anyone else, but might get work with short notice, or when I did get a job, a play for instance, then I was all in for however long it was. We couldn't plan anything, and he got tired of the disparity of income as well. Said I was holding him back.'

'He sounds like a prince.'

'I thought he was, once. Anyway, what about you? You actually *lived* in Italy, you lucky thing.'

'In Milan from eighteen to twenty.'

'Formative years. Have you travelled much?'

'All over. The US of course, Australia, a lot of Europe, China, Vietnam and Thailand, India.'

'Oh, my goodness, I feel very parochial now. Were you backpacking? What was your favourite country and why?'

It was his turn to shift uncomfortably. 'The thing is, they were all business.'

'*All* business?'

'Capital cities and business hotels and trips to factories and headquarters, fancy restaurants and boardrooms.'

'No sightseeing?'

'There wasn't really time.'

'How sad.' She said the words as if she really meant them, as if she was sorry for him. This unemployed actress who had hardly ever set foot outside her own country's capital city was sorry for *him*.

'Sightseeing always felt too frivolous, you know? There was always so much to do.' Why was he trying to explain and who was he trying to convince? Himself or her?

'So, no *"lads, lads, lads"* trips to Magaluf? No romantic strolls by the Seine with someone special?'

'By the time I was twenty my friends had stopped inviting me along on holiday. Our lives were so different. They were at university, barely responsible for themselves, but I was responsible for hundreds of jobs.' His voice trailed off. He hadn't meant to set himself so far from his peers, to lose touch with people he had known all of his life, but the chasm between their lives had been too great. He too serious, they too immature. Nothing in common any more apart from a shared education and the memories of his last carefree months and years before he had been catapulted into an adulthood some were only just now achieving.

'Okay, well, that's it. I am a barely travelled ignoramus and you are a well-travelled ignoramus so today I vote we sightsee like the tourists we don't know how to be. Deal?'

Lucas's hands tightened on the wheel as he

thought about his never shrinking inbox, the decisions that had to be made, the disputes to solve, budgets to approve, marketing plans to interrogate, a merger to complete. The Vineyard takeover was at a delicate stage, four shareholders had agreed to consider selling but none had yet signed, despite promises in Venice. He had thought today might consist of dropping Tally off in various towns while he took himself off to the nicest hotels to work until she needed a lift to the next destination. That he might join her for lunch, maybe a walk at the most.

That was what he *should* do. But it wasn't what he *wanted* to do. He wanted to explore small towns and hidden alleyways and medieval churches and see them through Tally's eyes, eat lunch in a cobbled square and watch the world go by. If she could find beauty and romance in an unremarkable Venetian backstreet, what would she see in Siena?

'Okay.' The words were out before he could stop them. 'We sightsee.'

It wasn't the first time Lucas had been to Siena, or Lucca or San Gimignano, but his earlier visits had been for specific purposes, for a meal with Roberto, or to collect him from a meeting or party. He had never before taken the time to really see the charming old towns, take in the stunning backdrops, beautiful architecture and preserved historic charm of these Tuscan jewels he'd previously taken for granted. But there was no taking for granted with Tally, who saw an adventure in every alleyway, a perfect view at every stopping point, a story in every shuttered house.

'How did Shakespeare conjure up these kinds of scenes when he had never travelled here?' she asked as she gazed at the fan-shaped central Sienese square. 'I know this isn't Verona, but you can just see the Montagues and Capulets stalking around on these cobbles, swords at the ready, eyeing each other and waiting for the other to break, can't you? Juliet behind shutters in a walled garden like that one over there.' She whirled around, clearly seeing the scene play out before her.

'I bet you are a brilliant Juliet.' He could envision her, impassioned and yearning, hair streaming down as she stood on a balcony, and what on *earth* was wrong with him? He had never been given to such flights of fancy before.

'I was always too tall for Juliet. I was usually the nurse, sometimes Lady Capulet. But it didn't stop me dreaming, learning the part in the hope I might get a sudden change of role.

She speaks some of the most beautiful poetry ever written, don't you think?'

'I don't know.' Once again, he felt at a loss, uncultured.

'"*My bounty is as boundless as the sea, my love as deep; the more I give to thee, the more I have, for both are infinite.*" You know,' she said a little wistfully, 'sometimes I quite make my mind up to give it up, find my plan B. Not because I'm thirty or because my idiot of an ex wanted me to, but because I've had enough of the rejection and the uncertainty and the constant desire to be doing rather than trying to do. Choose a plan B while I'm young enough to have a choice, to be able to progress in some sort of career. But then I stand somewhere like this and speak words that are five hundred years old and I know there is nothing else I'd rather do.'

'Does your mum miss it?'

'Not the very brief flash of fame, no, although I think the early part of it was fun. But to her the pub is the stage where each of us play our part, sometimes scripted. She puts on a pantomime every Christmas, and a Shakespeare festival every May—you might have heard of it? Shakespeare and a Pint? It's pretty popular. And of course she's queen of the karaoke machine.

She told me that she'd made a conscious choice, that she chose me and stability and Steve and that she regrets nothing, but you should see the way she comes alive, even in the backroom of a Chelsea pub on a makeshift stage, so I don't know if she's saying what she wishes was true rather than how she really feels.'

'You said you never see your father?'

'I've never met him and as far as I know he's never met me or shown any desire to see me. He has a very different life, made his own conscious choice. I could be angry or sad or have unresolved daddy issues and who knows, maybe I do, but my choice is to move forward with my life and to remember it's his loss. Steve has been the constant presence in my life. He adores my mother, he loves me, he's still housing me at my advanced age. I can't ask for more than that.'

'There's a lot to be said for constancy.'

'It's a bit of an unsung virtue, isn't it? Sounds a little unfashionable in a hectic twenty-four-seven social-media-obsessed world full of reality TV shows, but I agree. There's a lot to be said for it. Now, if I could just have a constant career, I would be happy.' She laughed but the wistfulness he had noted was still lurking in her eyes.

'Come on,' he said, not sure why but knowing he wanted to see her smile. 'I don't know about you but I'm hungry and Roberto has recommended an excellent restaurant somewhere near here.'

Lucas had no idea how it happened but that day set a pattern for the next few days. He rose early, worked through his outstanding emails and sent a message to Candace to rearrange his diary. Then, after breakfast, he and Tally set out on a sightseeing journey that took them into Florence for a hot crowded morning of sightseeing before Roberto joined them for a long lunch, for shady walks through leafy woods and several visits to vineyards, all with the beautiful Tuscan hills as a backdrop. Lucas didn't know when he had last been so relaxed. So entertained. So attracted. Tally was a ray of sunshine, usually vibrantly dressed, her mass of chestnut curls tumbling around her shoulders or held back with a colourful scarf, taking in every sight with an enthusiasm that was as welcome as it was novel.

The evenings were usually spent back at the villa for long dinners with Roberto, who was beginning to look a little better if still frail. They saw very little of Isabella, who apparently was enjoying a budding romance with a film director who had a villa close by. She arrived back late one evening, dark eyes bright with news.

'Sam is having a party this weekend for the cast of his new film and we are all invited.'

'Sam?' Tally asked.

'Sam Abraham.' Her tone clearly meant *Keep up*, but one of the many things Lucas was increasingly beginning to like about Tally was how little notice she took of Isabella's snubs.

'*That's* who you are seeing?' Tally's eyes widened. '*The* Sam Abraham? But he's a legendary director. I've seen his *Romeo and Juliet* more times than I can count, *The Draft* is seen as the ultimate Vietnam movie when everyone thought there was nothing else to say, and as for his adaptation of *Tess*...' Her voice tailed off and she sat, wine untouched, gazing reverently into the distance, occasionally murmuring phrases that might or might not have been names of films.

'You'll have to excuse me,' Roberto said. 'Once I would have been the last to leave but I think I have enjoyed my last Hollywood party.'

'If I had been invited by Laurence Olivier and Vivien Leigh to dinner, I would have no regrets either.' Tally smiled at him. 'But how exciting! Sam Abraham! He's a genius, and he always has the most interesting casts.'

'But surely you attend things like this all the time,' Isabella said, clearly surprised by Tally's excitement. 'You are an actress, after all.'

'If you mean have I been to the first night celebration and wrap party after a three-month tour of *The Importance of Being Earnest* or some other classic through small towns and theatres across the UK more times than I can remember? Then yes. But have I been to the Tuscan villa of one of Hollywood's most respected directors? Then no. But of course, we will stay here with you, Roberto, if you can't go. Maybe next time I get such an opportunity I'll be cast, not the guest of a neighbour.'

She laughed, but Lucas could see the yearning in her eyes. Of *course* she wanted to go. It would be like him turning down the opportunity to meet an investor or a brand he wanted to align with. She'd said she wasn't ready to give up on her dream and here was an opportunity to meet some really influential people.

Personally, Lucas could think of nothing worse. But this wasn't about what he wanted. 'I'm sure Roberto will enjoy an evening to himself for once.'

His friend looked up with an understanding

nod. 'Of course, there's a book I would like to finish. You young ones go and come back with all the gossip before I tell you about all the film stars I met in my youth and you will have no choice but to indulge an old man.'

'No indulging necessary.' Tally met Lucas's gaze and he knew that she was aware that he had agreed to go for her. 'We love your stories. And thank you, Isabella. I'd love to go.'

What was happening? Not only had he willingly spent days sightseeing rather than working but now he was agreeing to go to the kind of event he would usually avoid. Of course, it was important to Tally, a potential boost to her career, and he owed her thanks for the way she cajoled and indulged Roberto. But it wasn't just for that reason; if Lucas was being honest with himself, he liked to see Tally smile. To be the cause of that smile. And he had no intention of thinking about why.

CHAPTER SEVEN

THIS WASN'T TALLY'S first industry party. Okay, the couple she had attended she had been a waitress, hoping for a fairy tale moment where she caught the eye of someone powerful, was beckoned over and had her life transformed. And, to be fair, it had kind of happened, not the life transformation part but the beckoned over bit, not because they wanted to offer her a screen test but because they wanted another canapé.

But this was different. This time she was going as a guest and on the arm of someone who was a success in his own right. Tally hadn't realised, back on the Orient Express, just how much of a success. Hadn't realised that Lucas West headed up WGO, once West Gentleman's Outfitters, fifteen years ago, as he had said, the kind of brand found in the back pages of a Sunday supplement, but now the first choice for fashion-forward people with money to spend.

Lucas had mentioned that his father had left WGO on its knees and he had stepped in but Roberto had filled in the gaps, clearly bursting with pride for Lucas's achievements. It was Roberto who'd told her how Lucas was responsible for turning the brand around, expanding it. That WGO still wove much of the wool used for its signature suits in factories founded two centuries before. That Lucas had bought up other brands and other factories around the world to own a portfolio she could barely comprehend. That his designers and higher end brands had outfitted several films and plays, that stylists dressed award nominees in his clothes, that their invitation to the party tonight was as much down to Lucas's presence in Tuscany as it was to Isabella's ongoing flirtation.

It should have made her nervous, but instead it gave her a surprising strength. She didn't have to wow anyone, have a pitch ready, she could just be herself. Or at least the version of herself currently posing as the girlfriend of a successful and handsome man.

Tally had been grateful that she had given in to Lucas's insistence that she purchase outfits for all occasions including formal ones, otherwise she would have had to resort to the flapper dress she had worn on the train. Instead, she sashayed down the stairs in a red silk halter neck dress. The long skirt swished satisfyingly around her calves but her back was completely bare. She'd pulled her hair up into a messy bun, tendrils falling around her face, and matched her lipstick to the dress, emphasising her eyes with smudged kohl and lashings of mascara. Long delicate gold earrings, a cluster of bangles and a pair of high heeled sandals completed the outfit and the look in Lucas's eyes told her that whatever it was she had wanted to achieve, she had managed it.

'You look…' He stopped.

'Presentable, I hope, Tall?' That was what Max would have said the second he clocked her shoes.

'I was going to say beautiful,' he said softly, and the connection Tally was always aware of tugged deeper, harder, electricity zinging through her as she took his arm. Sometimes she could have sworn he felt it too. There was something about his hooded unsmiling gaze, an intensity that took her breath away. She was conscious of a satisfaction in how he sometimes forgot himself and relaxed with her—the pleasure she took in making him smile, in seeing that blue gaze warm with approval. But he had never acted on that warmth and although she routinely took his hand, touched his shoulder, slid an arm around him when they were with Roberto, she maintained a physical distance at all other times. Their budding friendship was complicated enough without adding sex into the equation. He might not even *want* to sleep with her and the last thing they needed was that particular awkwardness.

Although she was pretty sure that he was attracted to her in turn. But whatever held him back was his business.

Roberto had arranged for a driver to take them to the party and so, after promising to return with many stories and tales and to enjoy herself, Tally slid into the back seat, Lucas joining her. Isabella was already there, no doubt cementing her role as hostess.

'Do you regret asking me to stay?' she asked as the car pulled away and headed down the drive. 'I'm not saying that you were imagining things, but it looks to me like Isabella is quite capable of sorting her own love life out without any help from her grandfather.'

'Oh, she's more than capable, and Roberto knows that. He just worries. His health, as you see, is not good and if we were both single he wouldn't be able to help playing matchmaker. Just look at the way he keeps organising days

out for *us*. Yes, with hindsight, it was an un-
necessary precaution but—' his voice lowered,
as if he were speaking to himself '—but no. I
don't regret it.'

'Not even after four nights of sleeping on the
sofa?' she teased. 'I'm more than willing to take
my turn, you know.'

At that moment the car turned in at a pair of
gates even more ornate than Roberto's. Their
destination lay straight ahead, a modern villa,
all white and glass and undeniably impressive,
but it looked as if it would be more at home in
the Hollywood hills than in this ancient setting. Tally felt the first rumble of nerves as the
car drew up.

'Okay,' she said, more to herself than Lucas.
'The film is a play within a play, a group of actors putting on *Much Ado About Nothing* with
real-life events mirroring those in the book.
Real-life couple Xavier Pavez and Sabrina Rossi
are Beatrice and Benedict, ingenue of the moment Natalia Bennett is Hero, and teen heart-
throb Ethan Jones is Claudio. I don't know the
rest of the cast, they haven't been announced
yet, but we can expect stars with a capital S.'

'Which one is *Much Ado*? The one where
they get lost in the woods?'

Tally turned to Lucas, convinced he must

be teasing her, but he was completely straight-faced. '"The one where they get lost in the woods"? That's *A Midsummer Night's Dream*.'

'Right, so what's this about?'

'This is the one where the protagonists hate each other and are tricked into thinking the other one is in love with them by their friends. There's a secondary love story between Hero and Claudio and a villain, Don John. And you know all that—you're just trying to make me relax,' she finished indignantly. 'I *was* relaxed right until the moment we pulled up and I re-alised that there are people in there who could reset my career with just a wave of their hand. I mean, I know that's not why I'm here, but you would be the same if at Layla's wedding there was an amazing new young designer you wanted to sign. Maybe you wouldn't. Other way round. What would make you feel like your life was about to change?'

'My life changed irrevocably when I was eighteen. Everything I thought I knew about who I was and where I was going disappeared the moment I realised the extent of my father's debts, his neglect. I'll settle for safe, sensible growth rather than life-changing moments.'

'No one turned things round the way you did by being safe and sensible, but point taken.

Okay, let's do this.' She slid out of the car, so many butterflies fluttering in her stomach she was convinced there must be an undiscovered species in there.

Inside was as breathtaking as the outside, the villa built around a huge courtyard in which the party was being held. A bar was set out on one side, a long table heaped with delicious-looking food, along another, delicate lights giving the whole a fairy tale quality, as did the beautiful people in beautiful clothes gathered in pairs and small groups, lounging on sofas, under flower-filled arches, grouped on the side of the large fountain which dominated the middle of the space. A string quartet provided the backdrop and Tally hid a smile when she realised that they were playing a medley of theme tunes from Sam Abraham's most famous films.

You could take the director out of Holly-wood...

They had been shown the way by a silent uniformed maid who handed them each a glass of champagne before gliding away. Tally took a deep breath and suppressed the urge to press in close to Lucas. He didn't seem intimidated or nervous. His rather aloof air made him seem right at home whereas she would have been much more comfortable serving the champagne rather than drinking it.

Come on, Tally, you have every right to be here, she told herself, making herself stand tall and inhabit every centimetre of her five-foot-ten-plus-heels body.

It was strange to think if she had got the fantasy franchise part, everyone here would know who she was, there would have been a distinctive buzz when she'd entered rather than indifference.

But then again, if she had got the fantasy part, she wouldn't be here at all, she would be in Croatia, would never have met Lucas.

'Lucas, great you could make it.'

The thickset burnished man strolling up to them, Isabella on his arm, was unmistakable, imbued with the mix of arrogance, shrewdness and charisma that signalled an award winning and successful director. 'Looking sharp as usual.'

'Sam, thank you for the invite,' Lucas said easily.

'I understand you and Isabella are old friends,' the director continued.

'Old family friends.' He slipped an arm around Tally. 'This is Tally Jenkins.'

Tally took a deep breath, quelling her still

jumping nerves. 'Thank you for inviting us, you have a beautiful home.'

'Thank you. What do you do, Tally? Are you in the fashion business as well?' Sam's assessing stare swept her up and down, not in a sexual way but in the way of a man used to ordering bodies around on camera.

Tally took a deep breath. He might meet hundreds of aspiring actresses every week, there was no need for him to remember her after today, but this was an opportunity and she would be a fool to squander it.

'Actually, I'm an…'

And then she froze as a man came into sight. Early fifties, he looked a decade younger, although whether that was thanks to good genes or good work she didn't know. Her mother said good work, but then again, she would. Dark hair, with just a few flecks of grey, swept back from his temples, high cheekbones framing a famously sensuous mouth. Eyes the same golden brown as Tally's rested on Tally with no hint of recognition.

Indignation smouldered then flamed into anger.

He didn't even recognise her.

'I'm an actress,' she said, shoulders back, pushing any diffidence from her voice. 'But you won't have seen me in anything unless you have a particular interest in detergent commercials and the first five minutes of crime dramas. I didn't intend to make the first victim my speciality, but everyone needs a gimmick and that seems to be mine.'

Sam laughed as Sebastian Fields drifted closer. 'I'll look out for those commercials. Ah, Seb, do you know Lucas West? WGO? I wore a West Original to the Oscars and found myself in the best dressed lists for the first time ever. The man is a genius.'

'I employ geniuses,' Lucas said. 'I can measure a man for a suit, cut it and sew it, Isabella's grandfather made sure of that, but any genius comes from the designers and tailors I employ.'

'But that's the key, not doing it all yourself but getting the best men in for the job. Like Seb here, it took some doing to get him to play against type as Don John, but here he is and the film will be that much the better for it.'

Tally was so wound up she was sure she was vibrating. Time seemed to have slowed down, the air thick, every colour too bright, every sound too loud. She felt too tall, too vibrant, too out of place. The only thing that felt safe was being by Lucas's side, and so she edged close, taking his arm. She could sense him giving her a confused glance, her grip maybe too tight, but to her relief, without pausing or questioning, he reached down and took her fingers in his. His grip was smooth and strong, anchoring her, bringing her back to the surface and she clung on.

'And this is…Tally, did you say? Tally, do you know Seb?'

'Only by reputation.' The air seemed to clear, time start again with a dazzling clarity, all noise fading out until it was just Tally and the man who had broken her mother's heart and left her to fend for herself and their child while he took off to start again the other side of the Atlantic. 'But I believe you know my mother. You used to act with her on *River Close*. Charlene Jenkins, although her Equity name was Charlie Jenkins. Do you remember her? She's told me a lot about you.'

Tally's comment seemed innocuous enough on the surface but there was a bitter edge to her tone, subtle enough that only someone who had spent the last few days listening to her would pick up on it, her gaze just a little too intent, her hand still gripping his, tight and trembling. Something was going on here, a subtext he was struggling to pick up on, until he realised the

English actor had paled under his tan, that dawning recognition and horror mingled in brown eyes that mirrored Tally's own.

Mirrored Tally's own.

Conversations came back to him.

'The only thing you don't know that you should is about my father...'

A conversation yet to be had, the defiantly proud way she had mentioned that she had never even met her father, that her mother had ended up putting her acting career to one side, finding it impossible to juggle with single motherhood.

Sebastian Fields was Tally's father?

'Charlie?' Sebastian murmured. 'How is she?'

'She's fine. Better than fine. Great. She'll be fascinated to know I've run into you at last. I know she was hoping we would meet years ago.'

Tally's voice wobbled and Lucas knew she was close to breaking, to saying something she might later regret.

'Nice to meet you,' he said, squeezing Tally's hand reassuringly whilst making sure there was no warmth in his voice at all. 'Come on, Tally, let's get some food.' He steered her away from the entrance, and from the man staring after them, ashen, until he found a secluded corner with a comfortable-looking bench and deposited her on it.

'You okay?'

'I don't know.' She was shivering, eyes too bright, cheeks pale but with feverish spots of colour. 'I have spent the last thirty years wondering what I would say to my father if I ever met him and then, when it came to it, I didn't even throw my drink in his face.'

'Plenty of time for that, but it would be a waste of good champagne.' He took her still full glass from her hand and set it on the small side table, then slipped off his jacket and draped it around her shoulders. 'Do you want to leave?'

'I… Part of me wants to. But I'm not the one who did anything wrong, why should I be the one who scuttles away?'

'Attagirl.'

She looked more like herself now, colour back in her cheeks, the unnatural brightness in her eyes replaced by her usual liveliness, her back straight, shoulders back, chin up.

She was magnificent. She didn't need his protection.

And yet he wanted to protect her, to take up arms in her defence, to call her sorry excuse for a father out in a duel and fight for her honour.

It was terrifying just how much he wanted

to make her smile, to feel safe. He had never felt like this about another human being, Felix aside, before, not as an adult anyway, not since he had realised his parents' emotional problems weren't his to solve.

For the last fourteen years Lucas had had to have the answer to everything, but he didn't know what to do about this situation. So instead, he rose and held out his hand. After a moment she took it and he helped her to her feet.

'Come on,' he said. 'Let's show everyone just what a brilliant actress you are.'

The next couple of hours passed quickly. No one who didn't know Tally would have guessed at the emotional shock she must still be experiencing as she laughed, made small talk and entertained a circle of A-listers with stories of her life on the fringes of the audition circuit. Sebastian Fields didn't come near her again but Lucas was aware he was watching her, his expression dark and a little melancholy.

Eventually, they made their thanks and exited to the waiting car. Once she was buckled in Tally fell silent, almost unnaturally so. There was nothing Lucas could say. He instinctively knew she needed time to process what just happened. But after a long minute he reached out and took her hand.

He had touched Tally many times. It had never felt natural, he'd always been aware that he was playing a part, never found it easy to rub her neck or shoulder, slip an arm around her waist, touch her cheek the way she so effortlessly did with him. It made sense, physical intimacy was part of the actors' toolkit but missing from his. But touch was something they reserved for others, to show they were together, part of the lie. They didn't touch in private. Yet taking her hand felt completely natural, necessary even. Her fingers were cold, lifeless, and he held them between his, massaging the tension away.

To his relief, Roberto had already retired for the night by the time they got back to the villa and so they headed straight to their turret suite, Lucas grabbing a bottle of red and two glasses from the kitchen along with half a loaf of bread, some olives and cheese.

'You barely ate,' he said, setting some on a plate and putting them on the table before her, along with a generous glass of the wine. 'Here you go.'

Tally looked up from where she was huddled on the sofa. 'I don't think I…' But she didn't finish the sentence, her face crumpling as her eyes filled with tears.

'Hey, it's okay. That man is not worth crying over. You were brilliant.'

'I know,' she managed, but the effort of speaking the words only made her cry harder and before he knew it the sobs had turned deeper, more painful, as if they were being wrenched from her soul, and all he could do was sit next to her and pull her into his arms while she wept, murmuring words of comfort, he barely knew what, kissing the top of her head as she collapsed into him, her whole body shaking against his.

Finally, the weeping came to a shuddering stop and she pushed herself back, swiping at her face. 'I'm sorry...'

'I thought we had established you have nothing to apologise for?'

'That was before I went full-on meltdown.' She looked down at the damp patch on his front and winced. 'Your shirt.'

'My shirt can be laundered.' He picked up the glass and handed it to her.

'I just...' She stopped. Bit her lip.

'You don't owe me any explanation. You had a shock.'

'My mum was always really good about not bad-mouthing him in front of me. I mean, she didn't lie, pretend he missed me or would be here if he could or anything like that—she always said he didn't know me and that was a shame, but that if he did know me, he would love me.' She took in a shuddering breath. 'And then when I got older and could read between the lines, I worked out what an idiot he was for myself and told myself I didn't care. That I was better off without him.'

She took a sip of the wine he had given her. 'But at the back of my mind, I always hoped, you know? Hoped that one day he would seek me out and tell me he had always loved me, that he was sorry for not being there. I didn't want his money,' she said angrily, scrubbing at her still damp eyes. 'I'd see pictures online and in magazines. Couldn't help looking them up, even though each time it physically hurt to see him looking so happy. To see the villa in the Italian Lakes and the Hollywood mansion and his perfect wife and family at premieres, dressed in designer clothes and jewels and yes, it all looked nice, but that wasn't it. I just wanted… I wanted him to acknowledge me. To be proud of me. To count. I've spent my whole life feeling unfinished somehow, like part of me is missing, and it's not Mum's fault or Steve's because they are wonderful, but there's a voice who, in my darkest times, asks me what kind of person am I if my own father doesn't want to know me. Oh, God.' She half laughed. 'I really do have daddy issues. If this was a real relationship, now would be where you would run.'

'I'm not going anywhere.' The words were instinctive, from his soul.

Tally turned, looked into his face. 'I must look a mess. The mascara wasn't waterproof.'

'No,' he said hoarsely. 'You look beautiful.' And before he could think better of it, he took the wine glass from her hand, set it to one side and then dipped his head and kissed her.

She tasted of salt and wine and something indescribably honey-sweet, something uniquely her. Her mouth was soft and surprised and for one moment Lucas feared he had overstepped, taken advantage of her vulnerability. But before he could pull back, apologise, she melted into him, her mouth opening under his, her arms entwining around his neck, pulling him close. He shifted, pulling her closer so that she was half in his lap, caressing her neck, her exposed back, her hips, the line of her thigh, taking his time, getting to know her inch by inch, the silk of her dress cool under his touch, a startling contrast to the heat of her skin.

It was almost like being a teenager again, no rush to move to the next stage, no pulling of buttons or shedding of clothes, just holding each other, learning each other, tasting each other, torturously slow, every nerve on fire, as her hands traced the muscles in his back, tangled themselves in his hair, pulling him closer and closer until the tempo changed, sped up, heated up, a new urgency in their touches, their kisses. He half reluctantly broke the kiss, to explore the curve of her jawline, her tender throat, finding the sweet spot behind her ear, aware of her eyes half closed, her breath quickening, the silk under his hands now a barrier he was impatient to shift.

Tally placed her hands on his shoulders and pushed him slightly so there were a few cold inches between them and he stared at her, heavy-lidded.

'I don't know about you,' she said. 'But I'm ready for bed.'

CHAPTER EIGHT

THERE WERE PROBABLY a million reasons why this was a bad idea, but Tally didn't want to consider a single one of them. What she did want was to get up those stairs and get Lucas West naked. Her whole body was on fire, her breasts heavy, aching with the need to be touched, her mouth swollen with kisses, every erogenous zone standing up and begging for attention. And from what she had just experienced, that attention was worth begging for. Lucas West kissed like a dream, like kissing should be done as a goal in itself, not something to rush through on the way to the main course. And if that was the hors d'oeuvres she couldn't wait for the rest of the menu.

She waited, barely able to breathe. She had never seen Lucas so undone, his breath coming fast, his hair ruffled, his shirt half unbuttoned, his eyes heavy with lust. Lust for her. Tally smiled, relishing the power that lust gave her.

'I'm going up now,' she said. 'Don't make me wait too long. I need your help to get out of this dress.'

His eyes glittered and he was on his feet in one seamless movement. 'I'm right behind you.' Lucas's voice was so husky the words were practically a growl, vibrating through her.

It took every atom of self-possession she had left not to rush up the stairs but sashay, aware of the silk hugging her hips, the deliciously low dip at the back, her exposed skin. So her hair was a tangled mess, her eyes still red, her mascara smudged, this dress was seduction personified and Lucas was caught in its spell.

But that didn't stop him from reaching for her as soon as they were in the room, his clever fingers reaching for the tie at her neck, the zip at her waist, until the whole slithered down to pool at her feet, leaving her in just her lace thong and a pair of heels. His gaze sharpened, burned as he took a step full of intent towards her, silent and sleek and deadly, a blue-eyed panther and she his very willing prey.

'Not so fast.' Tally raised an eyebrow, wondering how her voice remained so steady when every part of her body was trembling with anticipation. 'One of us is overdressed and I don't think it's me.'

Lucas took his time looking her up and down, lingering on her breasts and the dip of her waist before coming to rest on the scanty black lace. A wolfish smile spread across his face. 'I wouldn't say that.' But he was already working at the buttons on his shirt, shrugging it off with languid ease, unbuttoning his trousers. Before she had time to take stock, to allow her greedy gaze to roam across the tanned, hard muscles of his chest, to follow that intriguing line of hair down his flat stomach, he was naked and stalking towards her, backing her towards the bed, which was at once too close and too far. She stopped as the back of her knees hit the side of the bed and he too halted, close but not touching.

'Are you sure?' he asked, low-voiced and serious. 'I know it's been an emotional evening…'

'I'm sure that I want you to stop talking and kiss me.'

Lucas's eyes glittered. 'Your wish is my command.'

Tally had no time to reply because his mouth had captured hers again with a new urgency as he swept her up and deposited her on the bed, his body covering hers, and then she was lost. Lost in the touch and the sighs and the moans and the sensations, in giving and taking and learning and wanting until they were finally joined and she had no idea where she ended and he began—all she knew was this moment.

Tally stretched out, aware that she was naked under the tangled sheets. Naked and alone, and all at once the events of the night before came flooding back. Her father, her meltdown, Lucas comforting her, Lucas kissing her.

Lucas…

Her head was a little sore, no wonder with all that crying. Her eyes ached, her cheeks still taut with dried tears. But more than that, her mouth was swollen, her body still tingling with remembered kisses and caresses. Who knew that under that aloof expression and buttoned-up shirts lay such fire? She'd suspected it but the reality had been more than she had dreamed of. And she *had* dreamed of it. Lying up here in a bed made for two, knowing he was just a floor away, she had dreamed.

But now it was the morning after. Not that she had any regrets. At least she would *try* not to regret anything. It was just she wasn't sure she could cope with two rejections in twenty-four hours.

Her father had made no move to approach her after that first introduction, hadn't even said goodbye. Not that she was going to dwell on him. He'd had his opportunity. Opportunities. Plenty of them.

The face that greeted her in the mirror was worse than she had expected and it took some time to restore herself to normality, spending far too long under the hot shower. Finally, she plaited her still damp hair and slipped on some denim shorts and a broderie anglaise vest top and steeled herself to see Lucas, trying not to catastrophise. He always rose early, she knew that, had always done several hours' work and gone for a run before she'd even stirred, and although she liked a lie-in, she wasn't exactly sleeping the day through.

But she was running late today, not surprising considering all the heightened emotions of the night before. That and how little sleep she had actually had. Her whole body heated at the thought. Look at her! Blushing like a fifteen-year-old seeing her crush at the school disco. She couldn't even tell anyone about it the way she would have then, analysing his every word, her every feeling, because as far as Layla knew, as far as anyone knew, she and Lucas were already together.

Sure enough, Lucas was hard at work when she steeled herself to walk out onto the terrace, but the look he gave her set her blushing all over again, stumbling as she reached the table and she saw his mouth curve into a wicked half smile.

'I trust you slept well?' was all he said.

'Uneventfully,' she returned sweetly and was rewarded by a rare low laugh as Roberto joined them, followed by his assistant bearing a huge bouquet of flowers.

'Tally, you must have made quite an impression on someone last night,' he said as he greeted her with the usual double kiss. 'These arrived for you just now.'

Tally's breath hitched as she glanced at Lucas but he looked curious rather than anticipatory, one eyebrow raising as he took in the extravagant arrangement.

'Am I going to need to challenge someone to a duel?'

'I do hope so.' Her heart hammered as she plucked the card off the top and opened it, only to fling it down, mouth pursed.

'They're from Sebastian,' she said shortly. 'He wants to talk.'

'Sebastian? Sebastian Fields? Why is he sending you flowers? Oh, apologies.' Roberto patted her hand as he took the seat next to her. 'I didn't mean to pry.'

'No, you're not prying—besides, these flowers aren't exactly discreet, but it's not what you think.' She took a deep breath. 'Sebastian Fields is my father, but he has never acknowledged me. In fact, I had never even met him before last night. Obviously, I had no idea he would be there, or I wouldn't have gone.' But the anger and resentment she had harboured for so long had ebbed, lanced by the experiences of the night before, those long painful tears, the long, sweet lovemaking afterwards.

Roberto stilled. 'Your father? Oh, my poor child. Maybe *I* shall challenge him to a duel.'

'No duels necessary, honestly.'

'And he knew he had a daughter? He knew about you?'

'He knew,' she said grimly. 'He was a teen soap star alongside my mother. He headed out to LA to audition for various things and my mother was supposed to join him once the play she was doing finished, but he made excuse after excuse, persuading her not to come. The reality was he wanted to reinvent himself, start over, get rid of his teen heart-throb soap past, become a film star and, fair play to him, he succeeded where many didn't. Meanwhile, Mum realised that her constant nausea wasn't stage fright or breakup grief but that she was pregnant with me. By the time she knew for sure she was nearly five months along. Sebastian made it clear that if she kept me then she was on her own. He would pay maintenance as long as she didn't put him on the birth certificate or go to the press.'

Roberto muttered something in Italian that sounded like a long string of insults.

'Luckily, Mum had bought a small flat so she wasn't entirely destitute and Sebastian did send some money, but she found it impossible to get work after I was born. A washed-up single mother soap actress is great tabloid fodder but not star material. Eventually, she gave up on acting but by then she had met Steve. She married him and managed the pub alongside him while Sebastian became the world's biggest star. It hardly seems fair. Who knows what her life would have been if she hadn't had me?' Her voice trailed away.

'Your mother is the lucky one.' Roberto nodded at the flowers. 'It looks like Sebastian has finally come to that conclusion too.'

'Maybe.' But Tally couldn't shake the lingering guilt that came over her whenever she thought about all her mother had given up for her. Oh, Charlene Jenkins had never uttered one word of reproach, she was always quick to reassure Tally that if she had to do it all again she would change nothing—*'Except I would be the one to dump Seb's smug arse.'* Her ire was aimed at the price of childcare, the lack of support in theatres at that time for mothers, the tabloids who had enjoyed documenting her fall from grace from the nation's sweetheart to abandoned single mother, with constant speculation about Tally's father until, thankfully, they forgot all about her. One reservation her mother had had about Tally's decision to start acting was that if she had achieved any degree of fame then the whole saga might have been raked up again and the speculation about her father started again.

Maybe it was a good thing she hadn't got the fantasy role.

'What do you want to do?' Lucas asked. 'Do you want to meet with him? Hear what he has to say?'

'I don't know.' Tally stared down at the note, at the decisive handwriting, the scribbled number, the two words: *Call me.* 'I mean, I do get the reinventing yourself part. I don't like or agree with it, but I get it. But he's had thirty years since to get in touch. He's got married in that time, twice. He's had other children. I have siblings. But he never reached out, never expressed any curiosity about meeting me or knowing me or even seeing a photograph of me. If we hadn't bumped into each other yesterday he would never have reached out. You know, I sometimes make extra money working the kind of events he attends. If I had seen him while serving him champagne, would he have still wanted to talk, or was it the fact I was with someone worth knowing that raised his interest?'

'He's the only one that can answer that,' Lucas said. 'But you are the only one who knows if you are ready to hear what he has to say. If you're not ready we can go back to London today.'

'You don't need to cut your visit short because of me,' she protested guiltily.

'Lucas rarely manages more than three days before the need to work lures him back to London.' Roberto squeezed her hand. 'I feel very lucky to have had him this long and privileged to see you pry him away from his laptop for so long. I hope you know you are very welcome to stay for as long as you want, but if you need some distance between you and your father while you think about what to do next then Lucas is right. You should take that time, however long it is. You owe him nothing.'

'Maybe.'

Tally did want to go home, she realised. She wanted to see her mother, see Steve, have some equilibrium restored. She had always thought that if she saw her father she would hold him to account, fire questions at him as if he was in *The Apprentice* boardroom, but instead she had clammed up, retreated, cried. Did she want that reckoning or, now that the moment had happened, was she content to leave it and really, finally put him behind her?

At the same time, she was reluctant to leave. What had happened after the party last night was so new, so unexplored. Sex wasn't part of their agreement but she had no regrets about what they had done. But she had no idea what Lucas thought about it, about her. If they went back to London, to their own lives, with occasional plus-one moments, did that mean there would be no repeat of what had been the most mind-blowing lovemaking of her life? It seemed a shame not to see if lightning really did strike twice.

There were too many questions she was too emotionally wrung-out to find the answers to.

'You're right. It's time for me to go home,' she said finally.

She tried to read Lucas's expression but

her passionate, open lover of the night before, her empathic companion of the evening, her only occasionally grumpy sightseeing companion had retreated behind his usual mask. And there was her answer. Last night was a one-off and that was probably a good thing. She had been promising herself a fun liaison, but Lucas wasn't the right person. He was too much in every way. Too successful, too rich, too handsome—just too damn much.

But how she wished he wasn't.

Tally managed some breakfast at Roberto's insistence before heading back to her room to pack. It didn't take long to get her stuff folded and put away, her suitcases neatly lined up. She was taking a lingering look around the room, at the gorgeous view, when she became aware of a presence, of Lucas standing there.

'Candace has booked your flight. A car will take you to the airport, she's emailing you all the details you need.'

'You're not coming?' She hated how needy she sounded.

'No. Is that okay?'

'Okay? Of course. Why wouldn't it be?'

It *was* okay, obviously it was. Expected even. So why did she feel so disappointed? It was ridiculous. Whatever last night was or wasn't, this had never been a co-dependency thing. They weren't *actually* together after all.

'But you're still coming? To Layla's wedding?'

'Of course. I promised. Send me all the details and I'll be there, making your ex so green he'll get cast in *Wicked*.'

'Good, that's good. Thank you.'

'Tally.'

There was something about the way he said her name that was hideously familiar. The tone was the one used for the talk. For the whole *Last night was great, I had fun, you are a great girl, it's not you, it's me, I'm just not looking for anything right now* talk. And although she was expecting it, she didn't want to hear it.

'Lucas, I want to thank you.' She jumped in before he could say another word. 'Last night I was emotional and a little tipsy and needy. Thank you. Thank you for looking after me, for turning something horrible into something really lovely. What we did was…it was fun, it was exactly what I needed. But it wasn't real, obviously. So do come to the wedding. I promise not to jump your bones.'

'I wouldn't mind if you did.' His mouth quirked into that little almost smile she was learning to really enjoy but there was relief in the depths of his blue eyes.

'I'm maid of honour. I'm not going to have the strength to do anything but sleep for twenty-four hours after the wedding. But seriously, thank you.'

'I should be the one thanking you. I had a really good time, Tally.'

'Me too.'

She should have felt low as the car took her away from the villa and towards Pisa and the airport. She was leaving behind any meaningful chance of getting to know her father and the sweetness and intimacy of last night, heading instead to the grim familiarity of a future with no job, no plan, no path, but she refused to let herself feel down. She had walked away with her dignity and her self-esteem intact and she had a hen night to plan, a career to continue chipping away at, and she had made her own decision to leave. That had to count for a lot.

She just needed the tingle on her still swollen mouth to subside, for the tender ache in her breasts, between her legs to ease, to stop wishing there could have been a rerun. She had a new wardrobe, had enjoyed a lovely few days in Italy at last and had experienced a night she would never forget. That was a hell of a lot more than she had had a week ago. So, no regrets, no matter how heavy her heart.

It was always jarring being back in London after a stay in Tuscany, the green replaced by grey, the sound of birds by traffic, the freshly prepared feasts by quickly grabbed meals, sandwiches on the move. Usually, Lucas was too busy with work to dwell on the juxtaposition, but this time was different. His house felt empty. His bed too large.

He'd done the right thing, or Tally had in the end. They had an arrangement; they didn't need to complicate things.

But he had enjoyed the complication. And now he missed it. Missed it a ridiculous amount seeing as he could count the number of days he had actually spent with Tally on one hand. Well, two, to be precise. Even including thumbs.

But there had been that one unforgettable night. He had been relieved when she'd pre-empted him and said continuing was a complication they could both do without. Relieved and disappointed. Who wouldn't be disappointed when he could still smell her on his skin, feel her soft skin under his fingertips, the taste of her lingering on his mouth, that honey sweetness with a hint of spice? Was it cowardice or

JESSICA GILMORE   163

common sense that had meant he'd let her walk
away? Lucas wasn't sure he wanted an honest
answer to that question.

So, it was obviously a *complete* coincidence
that his walk was taking him up and down the
streets off the King's Road, trying to see if any
of the pubs seemed familiar.

The Dog and Duck? No, that didn't sound
right.

The Moon and Sixpence? It looked tempting,
promising a courtyard beer garden and homemade tapas, but that didn't sound right either.

How had he never noticed how many pubs
there were in Chelsea before? Finding Tally felt
like one of those impossible tasks princes were
set in myths and fairy tales if they wanted to
win the princess's hand. Not that he wanted
to win anyone's hand. He just wanted to make
sure she was okay. Of course he *could* message
her—he had messaged her—but her breezy
'Fine' had told him nothing.

His wrist buzzed, his watch alerting him of
an incoming message.

Where are you?

Felix.

Taking a walk, why?

I went into the office and you weren't there. I know you're not abroad so I panicked. It's unprecedented.

Felix, it's Saturday afternoon.

Exactly. Unprecedented. What are you doing on this walk?

Thinking about a pint.

Now, why had he admitted that?

Ah! Say no more. I need to meet this mysterious girl of yours at some point. Roberto says you're smitten.

I'm not smitten.

I have many questions and you can't avoid me forever, big brother.

Lucas shoved his phone back into his pocket, unwilling to carry on the conversation. His brother was being overdramatic as usual. He wasn't *avoiding* Felix, not exactly, he just happened not to have been in the same city as him until today. He'd stayed on in Tuscany for a few more days before travelling to Boston to catch up with Brianna and a couple of other Vineyard shareholders. Now he was taking a summer afternoon walk through his neighbourhood rather than heading into the office. It was hardly the scandal of the century. Not suspicious at all.

Although maybe he was being self-indulgent. Maybe he should have headed to the office rather than strolling through London as if time was something he possessed. The Vineyard takeover was progressing slower than he liked despite his diplomatic mission to Boston, and there were always myriad tasks and decisions and strategies to review across all the parts of the business he already owned. Maybe Tally was right, he did need someone he could trust to take some of the load off. If only it was that easy. If only he could trust someone other than himself.

Lucas sighed, the burden he had thought he might shed for a few hours descending almost physical, his shoulders tense with the weight. What was he doing? His gaze lingered on a group of men around his own age gathered on pavement tables outside a corner pub, cheerful and loud and carefree. He couldn't remember the last time he had been part of such a group. There was no point having regrets. He *didn't* have any regrets, he had taken a bad hand and turned it into a winning one. He could have walked away, let it all collapse, no one would have blamed him. But he had chosen this life. There was no point complaining now.

And there was no point trying to do something different, be someone different. Better to return home, open the laptop he was carrying even on this walk, forget about tracking Tally down. He would see her at the wedding as promised but that was it. He'd find someone else for any other summer events he needed a plus-one for. Someone less discombobulating, less distracting.

Mind made up, Lucas turned round, his route taking him down a pretty narrow road he wasn't sure he had ever seen before. It was quintessential Chelsea, pretty houses painted a multitude of pastel colours, narrow pavements, quirky charm. Of course, once these houses would have belonged to craftsmen and retailers, distressed gentry and bohemians. Now, each one went for millions and were lived in by bankers. A pub took up the whole corner, a few drinkers spilling out onto the pavement outside the lead-paned windows. Colourful flower baskets were hung from the timbers, window boxes equally bright and cheerful added more charm.

The Duchess. It didn't sound familiar, but it looked quirky and inviting.

A chalkboard outside announced Pimm's, a refreshing spritzer menu and an array of bar snacks on one side. On the other a timetable: Monday pub quiz, Friday fresh pizza, Saturday karaoke. Private bookings welcome. Lucas hesitated. He had his laptop with him. Maybe a coffee while he tackled his inbox would be nice.

Inside was as welcoming as the outside. Low ceilings and small windows were enhanced by subtle lighting, making the whole place feel cosy. Tables were surrounded by comfortable chairs and benches, here an intimate corner for two, there a long booth for a large group, with flowers on the bar and on the tables. A second, larger room was visible through an archway. And there, behind the bar, just as he had known somewhere inside that she would be, was Tally, bright in an orange dress, her hair tied up, laughing as she chatted with a group of older men who inhabited their bar stools with the unmistakable posture of regulars.

She straightened and turned as he approached the bar, the friendly smile fading as she realised who he was.

'Lucas? What are you doing here?'

'I've been wandering the streets looking for a pint and a pretty barmaid to flirt with.' He hadn't meant to say the last part, hadn't even known that he had remembered the origin story she had concocted for them in such detail, and realised as the words left his mouth that if she didn't remember he ran the risk of sounding pretty corny. But Tally clearly did remember, her eyes lighting up with laughter, her mouth curving into a mischievous smile.

'I can provide the first, but do you think you can handle the second?' she teased.

Lucas placed both hands on the bar counter and leant in so they were close enough to touch. 'Try me.'

All thoughts of keeping his distance, of ensuring he wouldn't be distracted had fled. She was here and it felt right.

'Is that a promise?'

'Do you want it to be?'

'What happened to what happened in Italy stays in Italy?'

She was nervous, he realised. Nervous of what he might say or do. Had her eagerness to forestall his words in Tuscany been because she genuinely had thought it a good idea they put the night behind them or because she had read his intentions and wanted to get there first? If the latter he didn't blame her. Her father had rejected her, her ex had pushed her away. It was no wonder Tally was wary.

'I can't make any promises,' he said, low-voiced and intent. 'I don't know what will happen at the end of the summer.'

'I might have a fabulous offer and swan off to LA without a backwards look.'

'Leaving me weeping on the tarmac? But I do know that I haven't been able to stop thinking about you. That I didn't even know the name of your pub, and yet my walk brought me here today.'

'You haven't been able to stop thinking about me?'

'Did I say that out loud?'

Her smile widened. 'You might have occasionally crossed my mind too.'

'Just occasionally?'

'Every now and then.'

A group erupted into the bar, breaking the spell that seemed to be binding them closer and closer, and Tally stepped back, 'Let me get you a drink. I get a break in half an hour. We can talk then.'

Lucas wasn't sure how it happened, but he ended up hunkering down in a corner of the pub for the rest of the afternoon. He had his laptop and Tally kept him supplied with excellent coffee and occasional bar snacks. He was aware of interested glances, especially from the locals, when she came to join him armed with a mug of tea and a huge doorstep sandwich.

'I can do thousands of steps when I'm working,' she explained. 'I need to keep my strength up.'

'What time do you finish?' Lucas wanted to talk to her, but he wanted to do so alone, not under the watchful eye of a pub full of men and women who had clearly known Tally since she was a child.

'Karaoke night, I'll be on until close. But I am off tomorrow.'

Lucas managed not to look at his inbox, his to-do list. 'In that case, want to do something tomorrow?'

'Depends what you mean by "something"?'

'I've been thinking about all those walks in the park we enjoyed.'

Her look of confusion gave way to a wide smile. 'Oh, of course, before we reconnected on the train.'

'Might be nice to go for a picnic in the park.' Lucas wasn't sure he had ever had a picnic before, had never envied couples lying on the grass trying to keep their sandwiches out of the reach of out-of-control dogs before, but for one moment the reality was blurred by a picture of him and Tally, a picnic basket, blue skies...

'I didn't have you down as a picnic man.'

'I'm not, but you're bringing out my wild side.'

'Stick with me and you'll be suggesting sunset walks next. Okay, that sounds nice. Let me take care of the actual picnic part. At least I know what's needed.'

It was settled, they had a plan, although Lucas insisted that he be the one to bring the picnic. There was no reason for him to hang around and yet a couple of hours later he was still working in his corner, the coffee replaced by a non-alcoholic beer. The background noise was soothing, a contrast to his own echoingly empty house. It was strangely enjoyable to look up and see Tally at work, bustling around, laughing and talking, clearly completely at home. That made sense, it was her home. Even nicer to catch her eye, see the colour flood her cheeks, her intimate smile just for him, subtly different to the one she greeted customers with. She was clearly good at what she did, her warmth and genuine interest in people, underlined with a steely *Don't mess with me* core that kept the most drunken chancers at bay. Sometimes he was aware of her stepfather or mother not so covertly checking him out. She'd introduced them but forbidden them from any kind of interrogation.

A shadow fell across the table and Lucas looked up, ready to say that the bar stool wasn't taken and they could have it, when he realised his brother was standing there, an amused gleam in his blue eyes.

'Felix, what are you doing here? How did you know I was here?' he added.

Felix held up his phone. 'Tracked you. At first I thought you'd been mugged by an alcoholic when I saw where you were and how long you'd been here, but maybe you're the one who needs to go to AA?'

'It's non-alcoholic.' Lucas touched his pint defensively. 'I haven't been day drinking.'

'I know, hell hasn't frozen over yet. But it is past five on a Saturday so I'm planning on a pint of the real stuff. Do you want to put that laptop away and join me and tell me why you're working from your local instead of your actual office or your own comfortable study?'

There was no point dissembling, not with Tally within hearing distance. 'I can do better than that. Remember Tally?'

'Your avoiding Bella date?'

'That's the one. This is her pub. Say hello nicely or she won't serve you.'

CHAPTER NINE

TALLY WASN'T SURE how she felt about her worlds colliding like this. Lucas in her pub was discombobulating enough. She hadn't expected him to stay but it was nice, watching him work in the corner, feeling the weight of his gaze on her, looking over at him to receive one of his rare sweet smiles; he must have used a week's quota up today.

But it was odd introducing him to her parents. They would meet him at Layla's wedding so in a way it made sense for there to be a prior introduction. She didn't lie to them usually, but nor did she want to tell them about the deal she had made with Lucas so had mangled together some sanitised version of the truth. They had met on the train and when he had found out she had never been to Italy before he had invited her to Tuscany. They weren't dating, but were seeing each other casually. She completely missed out the meeting her father part of the trip; she needed to figure out how she felt about that before involving her mother and had managed to warn Lucas not to mention it either.

But now not only were her mother and Steve—and Leroy, Bill, Heather, Dev and all the other regulars—staring at Lucas with undisguised *What Are Your Intentions?* thought bubbles practically visible above their heads—but Lucas's brother was here, adding a whole other layer of complexity to what had seemed like a simple solution.

She could see the resemblance between the brothers. Felix was a younger, more relaxed version of Lucas. His eyes were bright with laughter, his expression open, his clothes equally exquisite but casual and he'd obviously perfected teasing his brother over many years.

'We can't go now, the karaoke is about to start,' he was saying as Tally headed over on the pretext of clearing their glasses. 'Isn't that right, Tally? Tell my brother he has to stay.'

'You say karaoke. I say my mother belting out showbiz classics to an appreciative audience,' Tally warned.

'Do you sing?'

'When she allows me to. But a few weeks ago I did "All Too Well", the ten-minute version, and she hasn't let me near the microphone since.'

Felix laughed. 'How about you, Lucas? Ready to wow Tally with the power of music?'

'You sing?' she asked Lucas, surprised. She wasn't sure she had heard him as much as hum in Tuscany, whereas she was always breaking into song, to her friends' annoyance. She had learned to mostly sing under her breath but once the radio was on all restraint went.

'Not in public. We really should go and let Tally work, Felix.'

'No way, I love a good showbiz tune. We're staying.' He winked at Tally.

Karaoke was always held in the large function room on the first floor of the pub. Hired out for parties and other events, it was also the stage for the pub panto and Shakespeare and a Pint as well as the weekly karaoke sessions. The stage was already set up and Tally opened up the bar, leaving Steve in charge of downstairs. She directed Lucas and Felix to a table by the window.

'Make sure you clap very enthusiastically,' she warned them as her mother shimmied onto the stage, resplendent in sequins. 'Whoops and cheers go down well as well.'

The summer holidays were starting for some

schools and this part of London was beginning to empty as those who could headed off
to second homes on the coast or abroad, but
The Duchess's karaoke evening was legendary and the room full as Charlene kicked the
evening off with a rousing rendition of 'Honey,
Honey' from *Mamma Mia*. Tally was kept busy
ensuring the singers and audience were well lu-
bricated, but when she had an opportunity to
check in on Lucas, she could see him watching
proceedings with a slightly cautious expression,
as if he were among aliens, but he didn't look
uncomfortable. Felix was obviously enjoying
himself immensely, already friends with all the
surrounding tables.

Despite Tally's teasing, her mother was a
good host who didn't hog the microphone *too*
much, compering expertly, supporting the more
nervous singers and managing to ensure the
more raucous ones didn't go too far. A couple
of hours in, Steve sent one of the other bar staff
to relieve Tally and she made herself a gin and
tonic and joined Lucas and Felix.

'Having fun?' she asked.

'I want to become a regular, where do I sign
up?' Felix asked.

'I'll send you the forms.' Tally smiled at Lucas,

suddenly shy. 'How about you?' she asked. 'Are you ready to join up, too?'

He didn't smile back, his gaze steady, intent. 'Maybe I am.'

'Come on.' Felix jumped to his feet and offered a hand to Tally. 'It's our turn.'

'What have you chosen?' She was half laughing, half protesting as she was dragged to the stage. 'I haven't warmed up.'

'"Don't Go Breaking My Heart."'

'A classic.'

'Tally?' She looked up into suddenly serious eyes. 'You won't, will you?'

'Won't what?'

'Break his heart.'

'His heart? Felix, it's not like that—' But her words were lost as he bounded onto the stage, the seriousness gone as if it had never been.

Felix proved to be a more enthusiastic than talented singer, but his spirited performance won him as many cheers as Tally's more tuneful one. She stayed on the stage as he left, arms overhead triumphantly, to take a couple of requests, a staple part of the evening, finishing with a pitchier-than-she-liked version of 'Jolene'—the karaoke at The Duchess tended to run to classics.

She took a bow and headed back to the bar, stopping as Lucas came over to her.

'You were incredible,' he said, low-voiced.

Her cheeks heated at the intensity in his gaze. 'I'm a little out of practice.'

'It didn't show, but it wasn't just your voice, it's you. You have a real presence. I couldn't take my eyes off you. I can't take my eyes off you.'

Tally's stomach dipped, her whole body flooding with a delicious, wanting ache, her gaze fixating on his mouth, so tantalisingly close, the memories of what he could do with that mouth weakening her knees. What she *wanted* to do was grab him by the hand and drag him back to her room, but there were limitations to sleeping in an attic room with her parents directly below—and working in a place where half the clientele had watched her grow up. Besides, she was closing up. But tomorrow they had their picnic date, and if it didn't end with them both naked and in a bed then it wouldn't be thanks to her.

'Maybe I'll sing for you tomorrow.'

His eyes darkened to navy. 'I'm counting on it.'

The brothers left soon after. Tally didn't kiss Lucas, or even touch him, but her whole body heated as he said goodbye. 'I'll see you tomorrow.'

'I'm looking forward to it.'

'Me too.'

There was something about his intent, un-smiling gaze that undid her, but, aware of their audience, she stepped back, trying not to show how flustered he made her.

'I'll warn you, I'm somewhat of a picnic expert, you need to bring your A game,' she teased him, and he looked even more serious.

'You can count on it.'

'Promises, promises.'

'Picnics, karaoke, day drinking. I don't know what you've done to my brother, Tally, but I approve.' Felix didn't show the same restraint as Lucas, sweeping her into a hug before clapping his brother on the shoulder. 'Come on, Cinderella, let's get you home before midnight strikes and you turn back into a fun-free workaholic.'

Tally watched them leave, her stomach churning. She had left Italy half expecting never to see Lucas again, sure that the night they had shared was a one-off. Seeing him again made her realise how much she had hoped to be wrong, how much she had wanted to see him again but had been too scared of rejection to reach out. Now *he* had sought *her* out. She wasn't sure what that meant, if anything, but for now it was enough.

'You look like the cat that got the cream,' her mother said, and Tally jumped.

'Good show tonight,' she said, trying to change the subject. 'You were brilliant, but I was a little pitchy during "Jolene".'

'That's because you were too busy mooning at that boy.'

'I wasn't *mooning* and he's over thirty—hardly a boy.'

'You know what I mean.'

'You don't like him?'

'I don't know him. But I do know from what you've said that he's an ambitious man. Nothing wrong with that, but in my experience ambitious men—and women—put those ambitions first. Like you, in the end your career was more important than your relationship with Max.'

'That's not exactly what happened.'

'Just be careful, Tally, that's all I'm saying. When two people want different things, someone gets hurt. I don't want it to be you.'

'It's not like that. We're not in a relationship, we're just having fun.' But her mother's gaze was too shrewd and Tally busied herself with collecting glasses, not wanting to carry on the conversation, or dwell on her mother's words. They *were* just having fun; nobody was going to get hurt and she was absolutely in control.

* * *

Tally had tried to claim responsibility for providing the picnic but Lucas had refused. He might not have picnicking experience, but how hard could it be to throw some sandwiches together? He usually asked Candace to organise any social occasions but pride stopped him going to his assistant for help, so he felt extra smug when he beat Tally to the appointed spot, a rolled-up blanket with two cushions attached to it under one arm and a not too twee basket in the other hand, filled with the best that a local deli had to offer.

He sensed Tally before he saw her, summery in a lemon jumpsuit, a matching scarf around her hair. Once again, she was as appealing as a long cool drink.

'Hey,' she said, coming to a stop a step away.

'Hey.'

'I know you said not to bring anything but I literally live in a pub.' She held up a wine cooler. 'It's impossible not to.' Her gaze fell on the basket. 'Ooh, fancy…and very shiny new.'

'Only the best for my lady. Shall we?' They walked companionably side by side along the pavement, heading across the bridge to Battersea Park. The sun was shining overhead and once again London had the frivolous holiday feel a sunny day brought out in the city. It didn't take long to reach the park and walk through, past many couples and families who'd obviously had a similar idea, until they found a secluded spot. Lucas set the basket down and unrolled the blanket, placing the cushions on top.

'Tartan blanket and matching cushion—very fancy and yet all at once traditional. Just what I would expect from you.'

'You approve?'

'I'm still reserving judgement.' Tally sat down gracefully and watched as he opened up the basket.

Lucas hadn't been sure what to get, so in the end he went for pretty much everything. Crusty bread, an array of dips and spreads, fresh fruit, smoked salmon and a selection of delicious cheeses, small biscuits and light cakes. The basket included real plates and cutlery, napkins and wine glasses, and he set them out on the blanket. Tally opened the champagne she had brought and poured it into the glasses.

'Cheers,' she said. 'To belated first dates and karaoke.'

'Cheers.'

Lucas couldn't believe how quickly the afternoon went. The food was delicious, the champagne light and moreish, the conversation even easier than it had been in Italy. They didn't discuss the night they had spent together but the memory of it hung there, not imposing but a promise of what might happen. What probably would happen. They saw very few people, although they were joined at one point by an exuberant yellow labrador who made a beeline for the picnic basket. Lucas moved with instinctive speed and managed to safeguard the remains of their food, whilst Tally managed to coax the excitable hound over to her until the owner finally turned up, breathless and apologetic.

'Is that the kind of dog you want?' he asked as their new friend was led away, not noticeably shamefaced.

'Beautiful, isn't he? I love them, but they're all stomachs, aren't they, labs? Not that I can judge, not after the amount I've eaten today.' She cast a half laughing, half rueful look at the picnic basket.

'Want to walk it off?'

'Sure, any destination in mind?'

'Yesterday I visited your home,' Lucas said a little diffidently. 'I thought maybe today you could visit mine.'

The offer hung in the air. He wasn't explicitly asking her back for sex, but he wouldn't deny that that was the hoped-for outcome. That he was driven to distraction by the memory of the feel of her against him, the sound of her sighs, the touch of her hand. That he couldn't stop staring at the place on her neck he knew drove her wild, that the only reason he hadn't kissed her yet was because they were in public and once he started he wasn't sure he would stop. That he could feel her gaze lingering on his hands, his mouth, his throat and he knew, without a shadow of a doubt, that she too was having flashbacks to their lovemaking.

'You didn't actually see my home,' Tally said eventually. 'You saw the pub, the flat is still unchartered territory, but yes, I would love to nose around your house.'

Tally insisted on carrying the considerably lighter picnic basket, leaving Lucas with the rolled-up blanket and cushions, an arrangement which left hands free to swing close together, to brush together, to touch and then to clasp. It was so natural, her hand in his. Their gait matched, swift but unhurried, and it didn't take long to reach Lucas's house, on a road close to the river.

'Nice location,' Tally said.

'Thanks to my grandfather. He was quite the sixties man and sold the Mayfair house he had inherited to buy here.'

'I mean, Mayfair is still a reasonable address,' she teased. 'But this is gorgeous, so close to the river.'

Lucas felt unaccountably nervous as he opened the door and ushered Tally in. Not because of what might or might not happen later but because he so rarely invited people back. Felix had a key but preferred his own Shoreditch flat, his mother hated London and preferred to stay in hotels on the rare occasions she was in the city.

He was conscious of Tally looking around, at the tastefully painted walls, the well-chosen art, the polished wooden floors, the comfortable stylish and sparse furniture, all selected by the interior designer he had hired several years before.

'I don't actually use much of the house,' he explained as he led her down to the basement kitchen which took up most of the floor. 'Just here, my study and bedroom really.'

The kitchen included a separate dining space with a comfortable seating area at the other end. It had been designed for family living but was also perfect for a man who lived alone. Why eat in the formal dining room when there was a perfectly good table or breakfast bar here, or sit in the huge and always chilly sitting room when he could relax in this comfortable space? Felix always said that he had carved a one-bedroom flat out of the four-storey, five-bed townhouse.

'This is nice, did you decorate yourself?'

'I got a decorator in.' He took the basket from Tally and began to unpack it, then took a bottle of chilled white wine from the fridge, poured two glasses and handed her one. 'My father used this place as his own personal party palace. Whenever I came here in holidays it smelt of spilled wine, cigarettes and perfume. I was always finding things that didn't belong to my mother, earrings or underwear.'

'Ugh…' She shuddered. 'No wonder your mother prefers to stay away. And no wonder you redecorated.'

'Pretty much had every room scrubbed and redone. Not at first, every penny had to be ploughed back into the business and I was in Milan most of the time of course, but as soon as I was in a position to, I handed the house over to an interior design firm. I should have sold it, I suppose. I thought about it but it was never a priority. I like the neighbourhood; I need a place to live.' He shrugged. 'It was easier to keep it.'

'Show me the rest.'

They took their drinks with them as they did the tour. First the obviously unused sitting room and dining room, although the morning room at the back of the house he used as a study showed more signs of life with filled bookcases and piled-up papers. Then up to the first floor. 'There are three bedrooms on this floor,' he explained as he opened the door into his room. 'Two in the attic.'

Lucas wasn't assuming anything, but he had certainly been anticipating when he had changed the sheets this morning, put fresh towels in the luxurious en suite bathroom, picked up flowers when he bought the picnic and plonked them in a vase on the dressing table.

'So this is where the magic happens?' Tally teased as she looked around the light-filled room.

'Not often,' he admitted, taking her glass from her unresisting hand and placing it on the mantelpiece before turning her to face him. 'As I said, life is mainly business first and I don't really like people in my personal space.'

It wasn't as if there was anything incriminating here, the house was almost devoid of personal possessions, or personality, according to Felix, but Lucas still preferred neutral ground, hotels or apartments, when he was dating. But he liked having Tally here, liked the splash of colour she brought to the monochrome spaces, liked the way her scent lingered on the air like a calling card.

'And yet here I am.'

'Here you are.'

'I feel special.'

He should tell her that she was special, that the thought of her had his stomach in knots, that he could think of little but her, but the words wouldn't come, so instead he kissed her.

Kissing Tally was exactly like he remembered, exactly like he had fantasised about, but still somehow new. She was summer personified, warm and sweet but with a hint of spice and fire. Her skin was silk under his fingertips as he explored her like a man who had been lost but was finally home.

He took his time at first, learning her all over again, tasting her mouth, her neck, her throat, the tips of her ears, tangling his hands in the heavy fall of her hair. His skin burned where she touched him, his shoulders and arms, his back, the planes of his stomach as she undid his shirt, button by button, almost agonisingly slow, her touch bold yet soft, sure yet exploratory as if she was rediscovering him. Last time they had fallen onto each other filled with emotions, she full of grief, he wanting to kiss her sorrow away. This time there was no baggage, they had nothing to declare except their attraction. They knew the rules and had decided to ignore them.

With a sound of triumph, Tally pushed his shirt off his shoulders and Lucas allowed her to slip it off, leaving him bare-chested. He kicked off his shoes but before she could tackle his belt, he turned his attention to the ties on her shoulders, kissing every newly exposed centimetre as he eased the zip down, her jumpsuit falling to the floor as she half stepped out of it, he half lifted her.

Lucas allowed himself to pause, to look at her, hair falling over her shoulder, clad only in a rose-pink bra and matching knickers, her eyes bright, mouth swollen, and his blood surged. He needed to touch every inch, to taste every inch, he needed to hear her cry out and know she was crying out for him. Her skin pinkened under his gaze but she met him boldly, surveying him with the same intensity, his skin tingling as her gaze traced its way up and down his torso, his blood roaring. *Mine.*

No more delay. With one movement, Lucas stepped forward and swept her into his arms, luxuriating in the feel of her against him as he carried her to the bed, letting her slide, oh, so slowly and, oh, so deliciously against him, every second torture and yet the kind of torture he wanted to last for ever until she was lying on the bed laughing up at him.

'What are you looking at?' she asked huskily as he made no move to join her.

'You.'

'Like what you see?'

He met her gaze. 'Do you want me to answer that or show you?'

Her eyes darkened, her tongue dipping out to touch her lip. 'Show me, Lucas, and maybe I'll show you in turn.'

'It's a deal.'

And then he was next to her, kissing her as she kissed him, removing the last vestiges of clothing, and the only words left were 'Yes…' 'Right there…' 'More…' Finally replaced by moans and sighs. And all he knew was her.

CHAPTER TEN

TALLY HAD NEVER had the kind of summer that could be montaged before, but this one felt like it should have a background tune to accompany idyllic scenes of sunset walks, drinks by the river, fine dining in fancy restaurants and picnics in bed. Of Lucas working from a corner in the pub, blue eyes resting on her as she worked, meeting Felix for drinks, a night out with Layla and Phinn, croquet in the park, a night in a countryside hotel. Bodies sliding together, entwined, touching and learning and knowing. She accompanied him to a polo match and a formal dinner, and no talk was made of arrangements or payment. It was simply natural she should be there and when he introduced her as his girlfriend there was no hesitation.

They were in a bubble, she knew that, a bubble of lust and desire, of sunshine and summer, but it still felt like it could be substantial, that they could be building the foundations of something. But there was no talk of the future, it was still so early, and although once or twice, lying cushioned in his arms, lazily tracing circles on his chest, she felt a declaration bubbling on her tongue, she swallowed it down. Tally had been too quick to declare her love before, she didn't want to make that mistake again.

She wanted him to say it first and surely he would. Surely that wasn't just lust in his eyes. He wanted her body, that was abundantly clear, but he liked her company too. Liked her.

'Off out again?' her mother asked as Tally walked downstairs from her attic room.

'Steve gave my shift to Tai. That's okay, isn't it?'

'Your choice. It's just I've hardly seen you all week. All summer, in fact.'

'Isn't that a good thing?' Tally kissed her mother's cheek. 'The last thing you need is your spinster daughter cramping your style. You should be pleased I'm finally giving you and Steve some space.'

'I love having you here, you know that.'

'And I love being here.'

'I just…' Charlene hesitated. 'It's all rather fast, Tally. You didn't even know Lucas six weeks ago and now you're spending every waking moment with him. You know I don't like to interfere...'

Tally fought to keep a straight face. Her mother lived to interfere. 'Well, I'm not spending this waking moment with him. I'm actually off to see Layla. There's loads to do with the wedding the day after tomorrow, and as maid of honour my actual role seems to be maid-of-all-work. I'm needed to chop and tidy and make garlands and whatever else Layla needs me to do. We've been planning for so long and now it's just two days away. Can you believe it? Those two crazy kids made it, just twenty-five years after Phinn first proposed with a plastic ring in the playground.'

'Feels like five minutes since you and she were playing Barbies upstairs,' Charlene sighed, her eyes misty.

'Or schools. I should have known she would end up being a teacher, she was always making me do maths tests.'

'And you were always making her put on a play. Give her my love and tell her everything is under control here.'

'I will.' Tally kissed her mother and left the flat, pausing only to text Lucas Good Morning. She had spent the night at home as he was busy. It was funny how quickly she had got used to seeing him every day. How much she missed him after just a few hours apart.

The day passed quickly. There were myriad tasks to do in the bustling, laughter-filled flat over the Lebanese restaurant Layla's family owned and ran. Last-minute rearrangements of the table plans, final tweaks to the table favours. Layla and Phinn had hired out the hall and canteen at the school where Phinn worked and Layla's parents were doing the catering, a mouthwatering buffet of spicy chicken stews, tabbouleh salads, a host of dips including their famous baba ghanoush and flatbreads, crisp falafel and a selection of honey-rich baklava. The kitchen was fragrant with spices, and Tally was put to work chopping herbs, grinding spaces and rolling out dough, just as she had been across the many years of friendship, the hours passing quickly under the weight of the many tasks this homemade wedding entailed.

The next day they headed to the school to set up, polishing every surface under the eagle eye of Layla's mother, setting up the canteen with hired in long tables then decorating them. Layla had chosen a colour scheme based on summer flowers, rich crimsons, fuchsias and magentas, vases set along the middle of each table, garlands hung around the room. It was a wedding designed with love, the modest budget boosted by the willingness of everyone who knew and loved the couple to pitch in. Phinn's mother and sisters arranging all the flowers, the bridesmaids polishing the borrowed glasses and cutlery, Phinn and his friends—not including Max, Tally was relieved to see—creating a bar area in the canteen and in the hall where first the ceremony and then the dancing would take place. Finally, the happy couple said their protracted goodbyes before Tally and Layla returned to the restaurant to carry on with food prep.

It was a relief to finally head over to the pub, along with all the other bridesmaids, Layla's mother, sisters, aunts and cousins and a mix of school and her friend's work colleagues and university friends for a selection of quiches and salads supplied by Steve and Charlene in the function room. It was the first and final chance to relax before the big day. Layla was staying at the pub with Tally, as she had so many times during their long friendship, the function room turning into a hair and make-up salon for the bridal party the next morning. Layla's dress had been delivered to the pub and hung in the spare bedroom next to Tally's dress.

Everything was perfect, just as they had

planned it back when they were little and playing dress-up. Perfect except… Tally surreptitiously checked her phone again. Nothing from Lucas. In fact, she hadn't heard from him in a couple of days, there had been no reply to her good morning, nor to the messages she'd sent since: a picture of the decorated venue, one of the simmering chicken stew. Both had been read but not replied to. Her stomach churned with a sense of foreboding. This radio silence was unlike him. He was busy every hour when not with her—and often when with her—his day filled with work, stopping only to go for a run or a gym session, but he usually at least responded even if it was with an emoji.

Don't be paranoid, she scolded herself.

Just because her last months with Max had been punctuated with unread messages and a lack of contact, even when they were in the same space, didn't mean that this was the same thing. Why would it be? There had been no clues, no sign that anything was wrong. She'd slept over just two nights ago, not that they had got much sleep, Lucas had kissed her goodbye, a lingering farewell, knowing she would be kept busy by Layla until the wedding and they wouldn't see each other before the reception.

There was an obvious reason for the radio silence. Lucas was probably working extra hard, if that was possible, so that he could keep most of tomorrow clear. The ceremony was at Chelsea Register Office, but Layla and Phinn would be repeating their vows in a humanist ceremony at the school before the celebrations started and although Lucas wouldn't be at the official ceremony she was expecting to see him at the second one, which meant he would need to take the whole afternoon off work.

Tally tried to join in with the increasingly emotional reminiscences as Layla's mother shared a series of photos of her daughter through the years and concentrate on the celebratory chat, but she was far too aware of her silent phone. Should she message him again? Just a simple Everything okay?

Was that too needy?

How about Looking forward to seeing you tomorrow? Something lighter, flirtier?

Communicating with Lucas wasn't usually this difficult, she didn't usually second-guess her messages. Her unease intensified. Maybe she should check in with Felix, but if everything was fine that would make her look like a paranoid stalker.

There had still been no contact from Lucas when the party disbanded—early, as Layla had dictated. Tally had bought organic face masks and a selection of luxurious body and foot creams and the two friends took long, indulgent showers, exfoliating every inch before lathering themselves in the creams and face masks and tucking themselves up in Tally's double bed, just as they had done for years. Layla had a large family with four siblings and had always loved getting away from the noise and bustle, whereas Tally equally enjoyed the opportunity to be part of a large, lively family. They had been friends for so long, knew each other so well, Layla would usually be the first person Tally went to for advice, but she didn't want to burden her friend on the eve of her wedding and so she lay there while Layla fell swiftly into deep sleep and resisted the urge to check her phone before managing a few uneasy hours.

They woke early the next day for coffee and a light breakfast before the rest of the bridesmaids and Layla's mother descended on them, the morning flying by in a flurry of makeovers and hairstyling. Tally went through the process mechanically, trying not to check her phone every five minutes, but the relief was overwhelming when a message from Lucas finally flashed onto her screen.

She really had to learn not to assume the

worst she thought as she opened it, only for her heart to squeeze painfully as she read the terse words.

Something has come up. I can't make it. Hope it goes well. L

No explanation. No apology. No endearment. No kiss. Was this some kind of attempt at a joke? Had Felix got hold of his phone? Lucas knew how much today meant to her. They had a deal! The terms of the deal might have changed, lines might have blurred, but he had promised her he would be here today long before she had developed feelings for him. Before she thought he had developed feelings for her.

It took every single acting skill she possessed to excuse herself without betraying that something was wrong. Tally made her way up to her bedroom and stopped in front of her mirror. Her leggings and her only half-ironic crystal-studded pink *Maid of Honour* T-shirt looked incongruous with her fully made-up face and elaborate half-up hair, the top pulled back to accommodate a wreath of dark pink flowers, the rest cascading down her back, more flowers woven through. It really was a work of art. With trembling hands, she took her phone out from her pocket, pressed Lucas's name on her fre-

JESSICA GILMORE   201

quently contacted list and listened to the ring-tone, heart hammering, stomach churning.

At first, she thought it would go to voicemail but finally he picked up.

'Tally?' His voice didn't sound like him, as curt as the text, distracted.

'Lucas? What's going on? Why can't you make the wedding?'

'I'm in Boston.'

'*Boston?* When? Why?'

He'd left the *country* and not told her? Okay, they had made no promises, hadn't defined what this thing between them actually was, but they were surely at the *mention you were planning to fly over the ocean* stage.

'Two days ago. The Vineyard deal is collapsing.'

'The…?' Oh, yes. The deal he had been trying to seal when she'd met him. 'Oh, I'm sorry. I know how much you've put into it. But Lucas, you promised you would be here with me today.'

It wasn't about Max, not really, not any more. It was more that it seemed as if he hadn't thought about her at all.

That she was the last thing on his priority list.

'Tally, this is a multi-million-pound deal. That's more important than some wedding.'

'It's the wedding of my best friend. It's not

just *some wedding*. Why didn't you tell me you were going to the States?'

'I forgot. Look, Tally, I get that you're upset but I'm busy. Can we do this some other time?'

Tally stared at herself, her face pale under her mixture of real and fake tan, at her eyes, large and hurt, her trembling mouth. 'No.'

She could hear him sigh. 'Tally…'

'We can't do this some other time because there *is* no other time. This is clearly not going to work, Lucas. I can't be someone you forget about and let down…'

'I warned you, Tally. I told you that I didn't have time for neediness. That I needed a partner who understood I might not be there.'

'That was when you wanted to hire me. But I am not on your payroll. A relationship has to be give and take, promises have to be kept. If something comes up, it's discussed—not sent as a one-line text two days later. I am worth more than this, Lucas.'

He didn't answer for a long moment. She couldn't picture him at all. He was like a stranger. 'If that's what you want. It's probably for the best.'

'I can't believe I almost told you I love you. I have to go. I have a wedding to celebrate.'

She ended the call and switched her phone

off and took a few deep breaths, willing the tears back. She would cry at some point, that was inevitable, mourn what might have been, berate herself for an idiot who fell for another man who couldn't fall for her in the same way, wonder why she was so easy to leave, but for now she was going to make sure her friend had the best day possible.

Tally's heart might feel as if it were breaking but no one was going to know.

Lucas hadn't seen it coming. He'd been so confident that at least two of the family shareholders would sell to him, turning his minority stake into a controlling stake, that he hadn't seen Hunter Johnson mount an opposing offensive, persuading the remaining family shareholders to consider his counteroffer to keep the company under their control. He should have anticipated it. Should have had contingencies in place. But instead, he had been distracted. Distracted by Tally. He had let his personal life interfere with his business sense, just as he had always vowed never to do. Too busy romancing and taking time out and off to focus on what was really important. The financial stability and growth of his company. The jobs he was responsible for. He'd been playing croquet while

Johnson had been counter scheming, picnicking while the deal was falling apart. He was no better than his father.

'I think I can be sure of Brianna, but I need one more person. I should have stayed in Boston until this was done, not wasted my summer in London,' he said to Felix that afternoon. Even as he said the words he felt a pang, a sense of betrayal. No one had dragged him to Chelsea, to the pub, to Tally. *He* had actively sought *her* out.

'Hardly a waste,' Felix objected. 'You are allowed to enjoy yourself, you know.'

'Not at the expense of work I'm not. My distraction could have cost us millions. If we don't have the majority share then our stock is useless.'

'True, but it's not the end of the world. Vineyard is a nice to have, it fits the portfolio perfectly, but it's not like our future depends on it.'

'That's not the point, Felix. Throwing money away is irresponsible. If I was going to mount this kind of takeover then I needed to be fully focused until it was through.'

'Tally isn't a distraction, she's a human being. A human being who I happen to think is good for you.'

'It doesn't matter what you think. She's done what I should have done weeks ago and ended it.'

'I'm not surprised. Standing her up at the wedding was a low thing to do, Lucas.'

'It's not like I had any choice,' Lucas snapped. 'Who else was going to salvage this mess? You?'

'If you ever relaxed your death grip on the reins enough for me to do so, then why not? Just because I don't work sixteen-hour days seven days a week it doesn't mean I'm not capable, Lucas. It's my heritage, my company too.'

'A company that wouldn't exist if I hadn't sacrificed everything for it. I worked my butt off so that you could experience everything I couldn't.' Lucas stopped, appalled. What was he *doing*? Was he purposely sabotaging every relationship he had left?

Did he occasionally feel a sense of envy that his brother's life in some ways had been easier, that he had seen out his schooling, gone to university, had friends and relationships and a work-life balance? Yes. But he also knew Felix's life wasn't perfect. He'd lost their father too, had also been sent to school far too young, his mother first emotionally and then geographically distant.

'No one asked you to turn into an emotionless robot, Lucas,' Felix said evenly. 'That's all you. Look, I'll be on the red-eye tonight so, depending on Customs, you can expect to see me some time after midnight. You don't have to do this all alone. But if I were you, I would be reaching out to Tally and trying to repair this, if she'll let you, which if she has any sense she won't.'

'The best thing I can do for Tally is what I should have done in the first place and leave her in peace. I'll see you later.'

Lucas ended the call and stared out unseeingly across the water. His harbourside hotel had amazing views over the ocean but Lucas was barely aware of what lay outside his window, just as he couldn't have described the hotel suite if asked to do so. He had stayed in hundreds of suites all over the world and after a while they had all blurred into one. Tally would have explored every corner, tried all the toiletries, sat in every seat and explored the minibar. But Tally wasn't here. She wouldn't be here again, not with him. He'd meant what he said. It was for the best—for both of them. She needed someone to put her first, to fight for her the way her father and ex had so singularly failed to do.

As he had failed to do. He had joined that unholy triumvirate of undeserving men. Lucas's hands curled into fists as he recalled the break in her voice. The moment she had said she had nearly told him she loved him. Now she hated him and he deserved it. He had been a coward not to tell her he was going to have to skip the wedding. It was partly because he had been swept up in the urgency of the situation, straight into damage control. But it had also been because at some level he had wanted to punish them both for putting him into this situation, for allowing his worst nightmares about what would happen if he ever took his eye off the ball to happen. She definitely deserved better than that.

He checked the time. Four p.m. It would be nine in London. The wedding would have turned into a party, dancing and celebrating. Her ex would be there, dancing with his new partner, and Tally would be alone because Lucas had broken a promise. There was no coming back from that.

But he had always known that this was his destiny, had accepted it. He was his father's son, there was no balance, and if his choice was a loveless workaholic over a destructive playboy then he was content with that. He just wished he hadn't hurt Tally in the process. Or that his own heart didn't feel quite so bruised, his life so empty and lonely.

It was what it was. He could sit here and brood or he could get out there, mount a charm offensive and do what he came out here to do. Win. No matter that he felt as if he had already lost.

CHAPTER ELEVEN

TALLY HAD BEEN here before. And last time it had been infinitely worse. She had lost her home, her future, her sense of herself as an adult all at once. At least, last time *should* have been infinitely worse. She had thought her heart broken. But it hadn't felt quite this exquisitely painful.

Late summer had soured. It was too humid when she went out, too stuffy indoors. She couldn't hear birdsong but the low drone of wasps zeroing in on her drink. Everything was too bright, too loud. She felt lost. Foolish.

How had she been so stupid? Lucas had been honest with her from the start. He was too busy for a relationship, he wasn't looking for love, so why had she forgotten the rules and allowed herself to fall for him, for the man she had thought he was? Because he had been kind to her? Because the sex had been spectacular? Was she really that needy?

She had been able to forget her lack of direction, her failure to forge a career those last few weeks, but now a sense of doom hung over her. She needed to make a decision about what to do next but was paralysed, aware how lacking her judgement could be. She couldn't even lose herself in the rhythm of pub life, her mother told her she needed a break and got the other staff to cover her shifts, but Tally heard her tell Steve that Tally was in danger of scaring all the customers away.

So not only had she failed at her chosen career but she was also tanking her backup plan. Great.

She allowed herself one long doom-laden week to wallow and then woke up one morning bored of herself and furious rather than sad. Lucas might have been upfront from the start, but he had still let her down. Broken a promise as if she meant nothing. A hot shower followed by a long walk along the Thames all the way to Borough Market helped clear her head, and by the time she reached London Bridge, she was able to take stock.

So she and Max hadn't worked out. How many twenty-somethings transitioned successfully into the rest of their lives? They had both changed since those heady early days when living on noodles in a studio flat felt bohemian, he getting more conventional with every year and every promotion. It was only with hindsight that Tally could see how much she had bent and changed to accommodate him. Would she really have been happy with him long-term, always doubting and apologising? Her biggest regret should be that the relationship had lasted so long and *he* had been the one to end it.

As for Lucas, he was just a summer fling. It had felt like more because she had been swept up in the romance and glamour of it all, and because she had really, *really* liked him. Had started to fall in love with the illusion and romance. After all, he had proved categorically that she had barely known him. The abruptness of the breakup and feeling that she had been played for a fool hurt, it would for a while, but hopefully time would give her some perspective.

As for her career…it was time to take proper stock. No more drifting and hoping. She needed to look at her strengths and weaknesses, what interested her and what bored her, and decide on a plan. A three-month, one-year and a three-year plan leading to stability and a place of her own. She couldn't allow her temporary living arrangement to slide into permanence.

And she needed to apologise to Steve and

her mother and tell them how grateful she was to have them.

Mind made up, Tally walked home, the return journey a lot slower than her furious power-walking there, stopping to buy flowers for her mother and Steve. They had the afternoon off and so she headed straight to the flat, finding them sitting at the kitchen table. Tally proffered the flowers with a flourish.

'I'm sorry,' she said. 'I know I've been the grinch who ruined summer, but I promise to be nothing but sweetness and light from now on and to make a plan to get my life together.' She stopped, puzzled. There were no answering smiles or understanding glances. Instead, both her parents looked unusually serious. 'What's wrong? Is it Layla?' Her friend was backpacking around Vietnam and Thailand for her honeymoon.

'No, no, nothing is wrong, Layla is fine. It's just you have a guest. I put him in the function room, I wasn't sure what else to do.'

Her mother was pale, tight-lipped. *A guest? Him?* Was it Lucas? Had he come to apologise? Tally stared at her mother for one long moment and then whirled around and darted down the front staircase, the one leading to the first floor of the pub.

She inhaled—*Be cool, Tally*—and opened

the door to the function room. The space always looked so cavernous and bare when not in use, chairs and tables stacked to one side, the stage put away, the bar shuttered. Leaning on the wall and staring out of the window was a tall dark-haired figure. Tally's heart began to hammer painfully in anticipation as he turned, only to lurch as she took in the famously handsome features.

'What are you doing here?' she demanded.

Sebastian Fields' smile was rueful. 'I came to apologise to you and your mother. I know it's too late, but will you hear me out? Please?'

Her first instinct was to flee. The pride which had sustained her through that awful party in Tuscany wanted her to walk out without replying. But the lost little girl who had grown up wondering why her father had abandoned her, who had spent her life seeking answers, who had put up with second best because she felt that that was what she deserved, couldn't move.

'Okay,' she said, her throat dry. 'I just… Do you want a coffee? Tea?' Offering tea, could she be more English?

'Tea would be great. That's the worst part of living in LA,' Sebastian said with the charming, slightly cheeky smile that had won him millions of fans. 'No matter what I do or what I import, I can't get a decent cup.'

Making tea took no time at all and yet for ever. She was at once numb and full of painful anticipatory nerves as her hands shook, spilling the milk, the situation so surreal she couldn't comprehend it.

'I have no excuse,' he said at last as they sat on two chairs, a table between them, untouched tea steaming away. 'Except that I was young and scared.'

'You think my mother wasn't scared?'

'Your mother is the strongest woman I know, and the most talented. I was in awe of her then, I am now. It's a shame…' He didn't finish the sentence but Tally knew what he was going to say.

'A shame she gave up her career while yours went from strength to strength?' Now she wasn't numb or nervous. She was furious and it felt glorious. 'It wasn't just the practicalities of looking after me, you know. Grandma helped when she could and if Mum could get the right job, she could have paid someone, but the issue was no one would touch her. Not for anything she wanted to do. Her reputation was dragged through the mud, it's as if they wanted her to be her soap character, not a real person. She

barely speaks about it but I've seen the headlines, front pages day after day, speculating on
her lifestyle, who my father was. Your disap-
pearance meant the tabloids assumed she'd been
cheating on you. One paper even ran a list of
possible fathers, all lies. No wonder she didn't
want to carry on living in the public eye. She
was barely twenty!'

'I know, and I am more ashamed than you
can ever know, I have been for a long time. All
I can say is that the longer I was away, the more
removed I felt from it all. My twenties were
as hedonistic as you would expect from someone with a lot of success and a lot of money. It
was easier to pretend that you didn't exist, that
I wasn't a terrible father, and the more I pretended, the more it became reality.' He looked
down at the table. 'I nearly reached out fifteen
years ago, after Phoenix was born. I held her
and felt this absolute rush of love, but also guilt,
that this was my second child and my eldest was
an unknown teenager. But Eva had no idea you
existed and I had no idea how to tell her. So I
went back into denial. But I felt that same guilt
when Autumn and Ocean were born, then again
three years ago when Sofia and I had Atticus. I
could never quite forget that I was living a lie.'

Tally had no idea how to respond. Part of her

was pleased he had felt guilt, that he knew he had been wrong, but that didn't alleviate the years of hurt.

'So, for fifteen years you wanted to reach out but didn't? I mean, you stopped paying Mum as soon as I turned eighteen. It was her and Steve who put me through university and drama school and it was a real struggle. A struggle I have never been able to repay.'

'It's no excuse, but that was the lawyers' call. I left that all up to them and they didn't even mention they were cutting you off. I will make it up to your mother, and Steve, if they will let me. And I want to make it up to you, Tally.' He leaned forward, his gaze intent on hers. 'Sofia knows all about you, I called her the night of the party. She wasn't best pleased, as you can probably imagine, and as soon as shooting finished, I had to head back to LA to see her and try and put things right. But although she's still cross with me, she's keen to meet you, if you are willing, and for Atticus to meet his eldest sister. I spoke to Eva as well and came clean. Not the easiest of conversations, she's not my biggest fan.'

'Maybe she and I could start a club,' Tally said, and he was startled into laughter.

'She'd like that, I think. Anyway, she suggested I come over and tell the kids about you.

They had a lot of questions and if the divorce hadn't put me in their black books, finding out I kept your existence a secret definitely has. But they are all excited that they have an older sister and all want to meet you, even Phoenix, and getting her away from her phone to say anything is rare.'

Four siblings, two stepmothers, all wanting to meet her. It was more than Tally could comprehend.

'And *I* want to get to know you,' Sebastian said, and for once he didn't seem to be using his legendary charm. 'So, will you come and stay? There's a pool house so you get your own space, a car you can use for as long as you like.'

Tally had no idea how to respond, what to think, her mind seizing on one practical consideration to give her time to process the last five minutes. 'I can't drive.'

'Everyone drives in LA, it's not like London, but we can figure that out. I know you're an actress, why not come out and try your luck? I can't get you a job but I can make sure you meet the right people. It's the very least I can do.'

'I need to think about it,' Tally said slowly. 'Talk to Mum.'

Her pride still wanted to send him away. Tell this stranger with her eyes that he couldn't buy her forgiveness with pool houses and opened doors and four unknown siblings and Hollywood. But hadn't she always dreamt of this moment? Hadn't she always wanted to know her siblings? She was no longer Sebastian's guilty secret, she existed, they were excited to meet her. And really, what was keeping her here? She had no Lucas, no job, no prospects, and her best friend was starting a new chapter whilst Tally was stuck at the beginning.

Saying yes didn't mean she was forgetting the past. But maybe she could move on.

Sebastian got to his feet and held out a card. 'Here's my number, my private number. Less than twenty people have this, it's family only.'

Her chest squeezed at that word—*family*.

'I'm heading back tomorrow but obviously you can come whenever you want. Just say the words and your ticket will be booked. I can't make up for the past, Tally. But I'll do whatever it takes to be in your future, if you'll let me.'

Tally watched him walk out, his number on a card in her trembling fingertips. What happened next was up to her. And the person she most wanted to tell was Lucas. Maybe the reason she couldn't tell him was the reason she should go. Start again. Sunshine, ocean, palm trees. LA seemed like the kind of place to help a girl get over heartbreak. She'd be a fool to turn this opportunity down. She'd needed a direction and here one was, offered to her on a plate, fate intervening. She just had to be brave enough to take it.

It was done. In the end Lucas hadn't been able to persuade three of the shareholders, including Johnson, to sell to him but those who did gave him a considerable majority share in Vineyard. His first decision had been to sack Johnson from the Board and install Brianna Wu as CEO so the transformation era could begin, his favourite part. The cut-throat thrust of buying and selling had never been the draw, it was what happened next that excited him. Vineyard had been resting on its laurels for too long— expansion, repositioning, focusing the brand, that was what got his blood thumping.

So why did he feel so flat?

Lucas knew the answer. It was because he wanted to celebrate with Tally. Wanted to walk into the pub and see surprise and delight warm her eyes as she nodded him to his usual corner. To flirt with her throughout the evening, knowing that everyone in the pub knew she was his, before whisking her back to his house to celebrate properly. But he had lost the right to do that when he had disappeared on her. When he had let her down. When he had allowed his fears to overwhelm him and blamed his feelings for her for mistakes he had made.

Clarity was painful. He deserved it to be because he had hurt a woman who had done nothing but enhance his life. A woman who deserved everything. But he had given her nothing. Worse than nothing. After all, he was the one who had invited her to Italy. Who had kissed her first. Who had sought her out back in London and kissed her again. He was the one who had made all the running and he was the one who had retreated when it all went wrong. He should reach out, apologise, but would that be selfish? She probably didn't want to hear from him ever again. He didn't deserve to have his conscience assuaged.

Felix was out celebrating with Brianna and some of the other shareholders but Lucas didn't feel like joining them. The humidity in Boston was getting oppressive but he didn't want to return to London either, to the big house he kept mostly shut up to disguise how alone he really was. But if not London, where? To Yorkshire, to a house held on to for family reasons although neither he nor Felix had enjoyed an idyllic childhood there? A house which always seemed to echo with the ghosts of his parents' arguments.

How had Felix escaped so seemingly unscathed? Lucas had obviously done a better job of protecting his little brother than he had realised. At least he had got one thing right. Suddenly overwhelmingly tired, he switched his phone off, put the Do Not Disturb sign on his door and crashed into a dreamless sleep.

Lucas didn't feel much refreshed when he woke the next morning, pulled out of his sleep by a noise he couldn't quite place, until he realised someone was banging on his door. 'Lucas! Wake up!'

It took him a few seconds to respond, then, shockingly wide awake, rolled out of bed and strode across to the door. 'Felix? What happened?'

'Lucas, why aren't you answering your phone?' His brother was in yesterday's suit, his face stubbled, eyes red with fatigue. 'It's Roberto, he's collapsed.'

Neither brother spoke much on the long flight back to Italy, but by the set of Felix's jaw, the muscle beating in his cheek, the fear in his eyes, his emotions were running as high as Lucas's own. From summer holidays in Tuscany, the highlights of their year, time away from the marital cold war that was their childhood, to his apprenticeship under exacting but kindly eyes, he owed Roberto everything. Roberto had even ensured there was a home for Felix during school holidays in those years after their father had died and their mother had moved abroad.

There were no direct flights from Boston to Tuscany so they flew to Rome, where they changed flights, arriving in Florence exhausted and jetlagged, neither having slept. A car met them and took them straight to the hospital, where Isabella was pacing up and down in a small private waiting room. Her elegant, freshly made-up face was a stark contrast to their travel-weary selves, but her eyes were so full of sorrow and fear that Lucas had no reservations about enveloping her in a hug. 'He'll be all right,' he murmured. 'He has to be.'

'You both smell disgusting.' Isabella wrinkled her nose but she accepted the hug, clinging on for a long moment.

'Over twelve hours on planes and in airports will do that. How is he?'

'Sedated. Go say hello and then I suggest you two go back to the villa for food and showers before we speak to the doctors.'

Lucas walked through the door she indicated,

his chest tightening painfully as he saw Roberto hooked up to a machine. The man who had always seemed so indomitable looked so small lying in the hospital bed, his breathing painfully shallow.

'Be bold,' he had always told Lucas. *'Set your goals high.'*

And Lucas had. For most of his life anyway. But he had failed this summer. What would Roberto say if he knew how Lucas had acted?

'Get better,' Lucas said, taking his hand. 'Get better and you can tell me off yourself.'

The next few days passed agonisingly slowly. Several times Lucas picked up his phone to update Tally but couldn't bring himself to send the message. She'd be worried, he knew, and it seemed cruel to stress her when the outcome was so uncertain. The three took it in turns to be in the hospital, he and Felix ensuring that Isabella went out for walks, for shopping, for cocktails, relieved when she bossed them around or sniped at them. A quiet, thoughtful Isabella was almost as worrying as the tubes and doctors' grave expressions.

Finally, they got the news they had been praying for, things looked more hopeful. The doctors would reduce the sedation and when Roberto woke up remove the tubes. All three of them haunted the hospital waiting room until they finally got the all-clear.

'One at a time,' they were warned. 'Don't overexcite him.'

'Thank God,' Felix murmured.

Isabella went in first and when she emerged ten minutes later her eyes were red but she seemed much like her old self. 'He's sleeping again,' she said. 'But you can sit with him if you want.'

Felix elected to go back to the villa with Isabella. She had a list of things they needed if Roberto was to be allowed home in the next few days, and the number of an agency which supplied twenty-four-seven nursing and personal care, and wanted to brief his assistant in person. Lucas promised not to leave Roberto alone and, after seeing the pair out, entered the small hospital room and took the seat next to the bed. The room was quieter with fewer machines, Roberto's breathing easier, his face less pale. He looked every one of his eighty-one years, but he looked like himself.

'I'm not ready to lose you yet,' Lucas told him. 'None of us are.'

It had been a long few days, and with some of the worry dissipating Lucas fell into a doze.

When he came to with a start, he realised Roberto was awake.

'I'll get a nurse.'

Roberto shook his head slowly. 'Water,' he said.

'Of course.' There was a cup with a straw on the locker and Lucas lifted it up and brought it to the older man's mouth. 'Slowly,' he cautioned. 'You gave us quite a scare, I couldn't cope with you choking as well.'

A ghost of a smile hovered around Roberto's mouth. 'How's Tally?' he managed.

'Good—' he started and then stopped. 'We broke up.'

'I'm sorry.'

'I don't deserve pity. I ran away, Roberto. For a legitimate reason, the Vineyard deal was in trouble and I had to salvage it. But I blamed myself. For being distracted. For allowing the deal to get to that point without seeing what was happening. I blamed her for distracting me. I… I wasn't kind. You'd be ashamed of me. I'm ashamed of me.'

It was a relief to say the words.

'Never,' Roberto managed.

'I've had a lot of time to think recently. I have worked so hard not to be like my father I have gone completely the other way, tried to jettison any desire or need for anything that isn't work. But that isn't living, is it? You managed to be successful and have a family you loved, and you lived. Look at all those stories you told Tally. All those things you have seen and done and felt. And my grandfather was the same.' He laughed softly. 'I can see the two of you now, out on the terrace with a glass of wine, planning your next adventure. Why can't I get that balance? Am I right, am I too flawed? Or is it just that I am too afraid to try?'

Roberto reached up and took his wrist. 'Do you miss her?' he rasped.

'Yes.' Lucas didn't have to think. 'It's like part of me is gone.'

'And you're sorry?'

'More than I can say but…'

'Then what are you doing here? Go tell her…'

'Just like that? Just go and tell her? What if she doesn't want to see me? What if she hates me? She probably hates me. She ended it, you know, but I pushed her into it.'

Roberto didn't answer, just stared at Lucas steadily.

'You're right,' Lucas said. 'As always. You taught me to follow my gut. Not to be afraid to take risks. If she's not interested that's my fault and I need to live with that, but I can't not try and make amends.'

He stood and dropped a kiss on the older man's forehead. 'Thank you, Roberto. For everything.'

He couldn't go yet, he needed to get Roberto home and settled, but he had a plan and, for the first time in many years, he saw the possibility of a different future. What happened next was down to Tally but, whatever she decided, Lucas couldn't fall back into his old ways. He needed to live, no matter how hard it was, to delegate, to let people in, to experience life outside of the narrow confines he existed in. He owed it to Roberto, he owed it to his brother, and most of all he owed it to himself.

CHAPTER TWELVE

'I CAN'T BELIEVE you're abandoning me to go to LA!' Layla said for about the tenth time in the last hour. 'I go away on honeymoon and you change your whole life around.'

'You'll barely notice I'm gone,' Tally pointed out. 'You know what this term is like. I hardly see you between all the harvest festivals and Halloween and Christmas stuff unless I come to a school fair or volunteer to help with making decorations.'

'It's just as we planned it when we were kids, me married to Phinn and you a glamorous actress in LA.'

'Out of work unknown actress staying in her father's pool house,' Tally corrected. 'But at least I'll be a step closer. Of course, I'll get there and my teeth will be too English and my hair too frizzy and I'll be two sizes too big and I'll be booking in for Botox and a breast lift and I'll still find it hard to get one line in a gritty drama.'

She laughed but she was only half joking. If she was struggling in London where physical imperfection was less of a barrier to success, how would she manage in image-obsessed LA? She cut her own hair half the time.

'You are perfect and you'll be perfect. Besides, you're going to get to know your dad. I am so happy for you.'

'He's sent me a first-class ticket,' Tally said. 'Can you imagine? Me in first class?'

'You deserve it. You deserve it all and once there you'll be far too busy to...' Layla stopped and clamped her mouth shut.

'To think about Lucas? I hope you're right.' Tally sighed. 'Every time something happens, I want to tell him and then I remember I can't. Heartbroken twice in one year. What does that say about me? The stupid thing is I was with Max for years, heartbreak is kind of the deal even if you know it's for the best and the relationship had really been over for a while. But I knew Lucas for only a few weeks. That was all. It wasn't even a real relationship, just...'

'Just mind-blowing sex?'

'There was that, but also someone who made me feel more, you know? That I could do anything, be anything.'

'You can and you don't need a man to do it.'

Layla raised her glass. 'To being strong and free and a kick-ass woman.'

'Says the new bride,' Tally teased as she clinked her glass to Layla.

At that moment her phone flashed with a message and, glancing down, her heart stuttered to a stop.

'It's from Lucas.'

'You haven't blocked his number?'

'I haven't needed to up to now.' Tally stared at the message icon.

'So, what does he want?'

'I don't know.'

'Open it then.'

'What happened to block his number?' With trembling hands Tally clicked on the message.

Can we talk?

She showed it to Layla, who rolled her eyes. 'A little late for that.'

'Agreed.' Tally typed the words and sent it.

'Good girl.'

'I know it was the right thing to do, but is it weak that I feel sick? That I want to hear him out?'

'No, feelings are never weak. What makes you strong is your actions. Oh, that's good. I feel an assembly theme coming on.'

Tally's phone flashed with a reply.

I know I don't deserve it. Just five minutes. I'll be at the park in an hour if you can make it.

'Which park?' Layla scowled as she handed Tally her phone back. 'This is London, he needs to be more specific. Honestly.'

'He means our picnic spot in Battersea Park.'

'Tallulah May Jenkins, you're not thinking of going?'

'I think I have to,' Tally said slowly. 'I think otherwise I'll always wonder what he would have said. It makes no difference. I'm off to LA, but I don't want to go with what-ifs hanging over me, you know?'

'Do you want me and Phinn to come with you?'

'My own private army?' Tally felt a rush of love for her diminutive but fierce friend. 'The worst part about going to LA is leaving you behind.'

'You need to stay there at least till half-term. I've got Phinn looking at flights.'

'Deal.'

The walk to the park was so familiar, but never before had she trod it with this twist of hope and fear. Hope that what? He'd grovel and beg her to give him another chance? Fear that he would be the same cold stranger as the one on the phone. Fear that the cold stranger was the real Lucas, the man she had known a construct. A one summer deal only.

Her heart stuttered as she spotted Lucas, looking ill at ease leaning against a tree, and she almost turned tail and ran, but forced herself to keep moving.

'Hi.'

He straightened. 'You came?'

'You said five minutes.'

She didn't want to prolong this, whatever this was, any longer than necessary—but, oh, he looked good, more dishevelled than usual, his hair ruffled, his cheeks stubbled.

'Right. Yes.' But he didn't say anything else.

'I see the deal went through.' What was she doing filling the silence? He *should* feel awkward, he'd *made* things awkward.

'Yes.'

'You must be very happy. I hope you celebrated appropriately.' Did she sound bitter? She didn't want to but could feel the anger creep into her voice, her stance.

'No. Partly because we had to go straight to Tuscany. Roberto had a heart attack.'

'Is he okay?' Her anger was forgotten. 'Why didn't you tell me?'

'He's on the mend and I didn't want to worry you until I had something definitive to say.' His mouth twisted into that distinctive almost smile. 'Which reminds me. He sends his love and says regardless of whether you send me away or not you are always welcome in Tuscany and to emphasise that he means it.'

'That's… I'm very fond of him too. I'm glad he's getting better.' She paused as she took in his words. 'What do you mean send you away?'

'Can we walk?'

'Technically, you've already used three of your five minutes but yes. Just not for too long. I have to finish packing.'

'You're going away?'

'No, Lucas. No more small talk. Tell me why you're here. I thought we said everything we needed to the day you stood me up at my best friend's wedding. The day you broke our deal.'

She started walking, glad of the reminder why she shouldn't trust him, of the surge of anger and hurt. He looked too good, too familiar, her hands wanting to reach out and touch him.

Lucas fell into step beside her. 'I am sorrier than you can know.'

'About what?' Tally hadn't come here to make this easy for him.

'All of it. Disappearing without a word. Standing you up. The way I spoke to you. It was instinct, the wrong instinct, I know that. One minute I was having the kind of summer I didn't think possible, not for me, the kind of summer I thought only existed in films. A summer filled with you. It became easy to clock off on time or early, easy to leave things to the next day, easy to take my eye off the ball. And then the deal I'd spent a year working on nearly collapsed and it was like the validation of all my worst fears. That personal happiness meant business failure.'

'You know that's not actually true, don't you?'

'At a theoretical level, maybe. In my gut, no. I always knew my father was irresponsible, Tally. I always knew he was a hedonist who didn't care how many lives he destroyed as long as he was having fun, but I didn't know just how reckless he had been until he died. How close we were to losing everything and what that meant. Not just a change in lifestyle for my mother, selling a couple of expensive houses, Felix changing schools, but so many jobs and livelihoods in this country, the pension scheme, everyone in the supply chain. All these people at risk because of one man's failures.'

'All those people are secure because of his son.'

'There was a cost and I willingly paid it. I thought if his eye was never on the ball then mine can't ever be off it. But this summer I allowed myself to relax and everything I feared happened.'

Tally stopped and turned to face him. 'I know all this, Lucas. I know who you are and what drives you. I can't say you didn't warn me. But why here, why now? What use is telling me all this? It doesn't change anything.'

'I was sitting with Roberto, and the reason I was there, the reason Felix and Isabella were there wasn't because of how successful he was or because of duty, it was because we love him. I remembered summer holidays in the villa, he and my grandfather playing chess and drinking wine. His wife, Magdalena, and my grandmother swimming or playing tennis, a house filled with love and laughter. My grandfather was a very astute businessman, he steered WGO into the computer age, shored it up so well that even my father couldn't quite destroy it during his decade in charge. But he had balance. His life was full in every way. That's the example

I should have tried to emulate. That's the life I should lead, if I'm brave enough to try.'

He took a deep breath. 'I'm sorrier than you can know, Tally. I pushed you away not because I blamed you but because I blamed myself for falling for you. For starting to love you. Somehow, I thought loving was weak, but that's not true, is it? Daring to love is the bravest thing a person can do. I love you, Tally. I just needed to tell you that.'

Tally stopped still, her feet refusing to keep walking, her mind whirling with all he had said, circling around over and over to those three words. He loved her. And she loved him. That was why he'd been able to hurt her so badly. And that was why she wasn't sure she would be able to trust him with her heart again, however much she wanted to.

'I'm going to LA,' she blurted out. 'I don't know for how long—my father has got me an artist's visa somehow. But for a while. I leave in two days. Tonight's karaoke is my send-off party.'

She reached out and took his hand, his fingers warm in hers, so achingly familiar she wanted to cling on for ever. Instead, she squeezed and let it drop again.

'I knew,' she said simply. 'Not that you...'

She couldn't quite bring herself to say love. 'Not that you had feelings for me, but the rest. You've told me enough for me to guess and I know you, Lucas. Know that despite what you did you're a good man, just one with scars. We all bear them. Look at me, so frightened of being left I clung onto a relationship long after it should have been put out of its misery and then wallowed for months after. But I've made a decision. I won't allow anyone to define happiness for me again. I'm worth more than that. I fell for you too, Lucas. I think maybe I loved you too. But although I understand why you did what you did, you still hurt me. You still did the one thing you knew I wasn't equipped to handle. So I can't trust you and without trust there can't be a future. I do appreciate you telling me all this, I know it couldn't have been easy. But there's nowhere for us to go. Give my love to Felix and Roberto.'

She allowed herself to touch his cheek. Just once. And then she turned and left. Heart breaking once again, part convinced she was making a terrible mistake but knowing deep inside it was the only way.

'How did it go?'

Felix's voice was loud and exuberant and Lucas winced.

'Not good. She's going to LA and will never trust me again.'

'LA? To see her father? How did that come about?'

'I don't know. We didn't really do small talk.'

'It's a *huge* thing, how is that small talk?'

'I was too busy humbling myself to ask, if you must know. But she made it quite clear she doesn't want to see me again and I have to respect that, Felix.'

At some point this numbness would wear off and then he would hurt, a lot. It would hurt more knowing he had brought this on himself.

'I can't trust you,' she had said.

He had prided himself on his integrity, on being a good guy, not a player like his father, and yet here he was.

'So, you're just giving up?'

'No, I'm respecting her boundaries. What do you want me to do? Ambush her at the airport? Follow her to LA? Get arrested for stalking?'

'When does she go?'

'Monday.'

'Tonight's karaoke night.'

'Yes, her farewell party, she said.'

'Perfect! That's your chance.'

'My what?' His brother's meaning dawned. 'We can't just turn up. We're probably barred.'

'*You're* probably barred. There's no need to bar me.'

'And do what? Sing my apologies to her?'

'You hurt her, Lucas, humiliated her. You need to humiliate yourself to even things out.'

Lucas narrowed his eyes. 'You just want to make me sing, don't you?'

'I would give a year's salary to watch you apologise in musical form.'

Lucas almost—almost—laughed at the glee in his brother's voice.

'This is my future, Felix. You're right, if I don't try again, I *am* giving up. Tally doesn't trust me and if I give up then I guess I am just agreeing with her that I can't change, that what we have isn't worth repairing. But trust isn't something I can just conjure up. It has to be proven over time. No one gesture, no matter how humiliating or heartfelt, can do that.'

'I agree, but I'm not the one you need to say that to. And for the record, I think a humiliating gesture will help. Not that I'm at all biased. I'll see you this evening. I can shield you from the angry locals.'

'More likely to run away and leave me to face the pitchforks.'

'That too. See you later.'

Lucas ended the call feeling marginally better. He had never just given up in his life and he wasn't about to start now. What he and Tally had had, could have, was more than worth another try, and if he had to humiliate himself in the process then that was a small price to pay.

Despite Felix's urging Lucas didn't want to show up at the beginning of the evening. It wasn't that he was afraid to walk into a room full of people who probably wanted to tear him limb from limb, it was that this was Tally's night, her chance to shine, her goodbye, and he didn't want to take a second of that away from her. Grand gestures were all very well but if you were going to take over someone else's occasion you had to be very sure they wanted you to. And he wasn't sure at all.

He met Felix for dinner first, although he could barely swallow a bite of what he knew was an excellent steak, could barely finish the one glass of red wine, his mind racing with a dozen different permutations of how the evening might end, from being thrown out of The Duchess before getting to say one word to sweeping Tally up in his arms and carrying her all the way back to his. Either seemed as likely.

'Come on, big bro,' Felix said eventually. 'Let's go get your girl.'

The walk to the pub seemed to take for ever,

and yet they were there impossibly fast. The downstairs was unusually quiet and, to his relief, Lucas didn't recognise the people behind the bar. He and Felix made their way up to the function room and slipped quietly into the crowded space. No one noticed them come in, the lights were turned down and most people were facing the stage the other side of the room, where Charlene was performing an emotional cover of 'Slipping Through my Fingers'.

Lucas took up a position in a dark corner as Felix slipped away to get them both a pint and watched as Tally retook the microphone and treated them to several requests. She was dazzling, holding the crowd in the palm of her hand, her voice true and sweet with a rich timbre that was all hers. She had *it*, whatever that indefinable it was, and Lucas realised that if she got the opportunity she deserved then she might be in LA for some time. For a moment he considered disappearing out as quietly as he had come, leaving her to get on with her new life. But it didn't have to be one or the other. She should have it all and if he was lucky enough for that to include him then there was always a way.

Finally, the evening came to a close. Steve and Charlene made short emotional speeches and Tally, through tears, thanked them for everything. People started to filter out after hugging Tally, many leaving presents and cards. Lucas hung back, not wanting to interrupt just yet. In the end it was just Layla, Phinn and her family, Steve and Charlene and a smattering of other people he recognised.

It was time.

'Wish me luck,' Lucas muttered to Felix and stepped out of his corner.

Tally didn't think her emotions could get any more heightened. She'd been filled with a mixture of excitement and trepidation before seeing Lucas this morning, afterwards filled with doubt and sadness. Walking away had been almost unbearably hard even though she knew it was the right thing to do. Now she was surrounded by people who loved her, who supported her, and she had to say goodbye. No matter that she kept telling herself that LA was an eleven-hour flight away and she could come back for a visit at any time, that she might hate it, that she might return in just a few weeks, it still felt like the end of an era. She'd channelled all those feelings into her performance, even though it was just a makeshift stage in a small pub, and she knew her mother had done the same. She owed Charlene a lot, but her mother's unwavering belief in Tally and reassurance that moving to LA and getting to know her father was the right thing to do was her mother's most selfless act yet.

How she was going to say goodbye on Monday she didn't know.

She approached Layla and Phinn but, before she could speak, she was aware of someone walking towards her.

Lucas.

'What's he doing here?' Layla hissed.

To anyone who didn't know Lucas he probably looked supremely at ease, but Tally could see telltale signs that he wasn't as confident as he appeared. His jaw was set, a muscle beating in his cheek, his expression shadowed.

'Am I too late?'

'You were too late weeks ago,' Layla said, arms folded.

'Too late for what? You already apologised,' Tally said.

Lucas nodded towards the stage. 'To sing.'

'To *what*?' Was she dreaming? This was getting more surreal by the moment. 'I…'

'No,' her mother said, and Tally glanced at her in surprise. Charlene also had her arms folded and her expression was forbidding. 'You're not too late.'

'Right then.' Lucas made his way purposefully to the stage.

'You don't have to,' she half whispered as he passed her and he gave her the half-smile she loved.

'I know. I want to. Unless you would prefer I didn't?'

'I…' But of course she was curious. 'Be my guest.'

Lucas took some time choosing then came to stand in the middle of the stage. 'I'm not here to hijack Tally's evening,' he said. 'Nor am I here to beg her to reconsider. But I do want her to know how very sorry I am. Felix said the best way would be for me to humiliate myself, but I don't see this as humiliation, I see it as speaking Tally's language. Okay, then…'

For a moment he looked unsure, then squared his shoulders and attraction rippled through her.

Tally stood where she was, surrounded by people who loved her, anticipation coursing through her. She didn't mind a bad performance musically as long as the singer committed. Lucas certainly *looked* like he knew what he was doing, the microphone held loosely in one hand as he waited for the music to start. What would he sing? Something croony? Rock? Pop?

Please don't let him try and rap.

To her shock, a guitar began to fill the room. Surely it wasn't…? Not *Elvis*?

Lucas began to sing 'Heartbreak Hotel'. He didn't fall into the trap of trying to mimic Elvis, a pitfall she had seen many a karaoke singer fall into, but sang the sweet, deceptively simple song straight, imbuing the well-known lyrics and tune with a pathos she hadn't heard before. His voice wasn't the strongest, but it was true and held the room spellbound through the short song, and the smattering of applause at the end was heartfelt.

'I miss you, Tally,' he said. 'I let you down, badly, and no amount of apologies and impromptu performances can fix that. I know you don't trust me and I understand why. I'm not asking you to take me back…' Was that *disappointment* she felt? 'And I am certainly not going to ask you not to go to LA, you absolutely should. But I am asking you to let me prove that I can change, that I have changed. I can't promise not to be a workaholic and I can't promise not to bear my responsibilities heavily, although I can allow Felix to shoulder some of them. But I can promise to put you first, if you'll let me. I want to date you, Tallulah Jenkins. Slowly, steadily, properly. Rebuild that trust, show you that I can be the man you deserve. Show you how much I love you.' He stopped then and stood there, heart in his eyes.

Tally looked around and realised that her family and friends had left them alone. She'd been too caught up in Lucas's words to notice.

'You are full of surprises, Lucas West,' she said.

'I'm trying.' He jumped down from the stage and made his way towards her until he was standing in front of her.

'You want to date me?'

'I'll be spending more time in Boston and New York. I can come to you, maybe you can come to me. We can talk on the phone in between visits, start again, start properly. I love you, Tally, I think I have loved you since you burst into my compartment in the Orient Express, since you bought me a coffee in a backstreet in Venice and looked around as if you were in the most beautiful square. I love your tenacity and the joy you find in everyday things; I love your heart and your talent. I know I don't deserve you but...'

She put a finger up to his mouth. 'I love you too,' she said and it was a relief to say the words. 'Not because you sang to me, although that was amazing, but because you are you. A man who cares too much, who thinks he doesn't deserve happiness. I'm not sure what the future holds, but I do want you to be in it. I want to see what we could be if we start again. If we date.'

Date. Such an old-fashioned word and yet one that encompassed so much. Hope and possibility and second chances.

'I love you, Tally.'

'I love you too.'

And as he kissed her, she knew she was making the right choice. The future was full of uncertainties, but she had to take a chance on happiness.

EPILOGUE

One year later

'YOU'RE HERE!' TALLY RACED along the beach towards Lucas's tall figure. 'I wasn't expecting you until tomorrow.'

'It's our first night in our new house, where else could I be?' He swept her into his arms and she leaned into his kiss, luxuriating in the feel of him.

'I can't believe it's ours.' Tally looked back at the gorgeous Malibu beach house. 'When I walked inside, I half expected someone to tell me it was all a joke and escort me out. My clothes barely fill a tenth of that dressing room.'

'How's work?'

Tally loved the pride in Lucas's smile as he asked the question. He had been as excited as she had when she had landed a recurring role on a new hospital drama, playing an English doctor.

'Good! I feel like I'm learning every day, just being on set is a dream.' Her days were long but she wasn't complaining. Best of all, she had landed the role on her own—the producers had had no idea who her father was when they'd hired her, that news was still very much under wraps.

It had been an incredible year, from forging a relationship with her father and siblings, to landing the job of her dreams, to buying the house with Lucas. As promised, they'd taken things slowly for a few months, meals out and daytrips leading to weekend breaks and holidays, until Lucas started spending more and more time in LA. A couple of months ago he had leased office space in the city and the pair had started to house hunt. Now here they were, owners of the kind of house she used to daydream about.

'Maybe it's time to consider that dog,' she suggested.

'Do you think we're ready for that kind of commitment?'

'We do own a house together.'

'That's true. But there's one more step we could take.' To her shock, he fell to one knee, a small box in his hands. 'Tallulah May Jenkins, I can't believe I'm here with you, that you took pity on me and allowed me a second chance, that we have a house and a life together. The only thing that could make me happier is if you marry me. Will you, Tally?'

'Get up! Of course. Oh, it's beautiful,' as he opened the box to display a diamond set emerald ring. 'I love it.'

'I saw it in Venice when we were there last month and it made me think of you. You mean it?' He slid the ring onto her finger. 'It's a yes?'

'Does this mean we can get a dog?'

'A whole pack if you say yes,' he promised recklessly, and she laughed.

'Let's start with one. I love you, Lucas.'

'I love you too.'

'We should get married in Tuscany, so Roberto can be there.'

'And honeymoon on the Orient Express?'

'Back where it all began. Perfect.'

Tally lost herself in his kiss, in the man she loved, with the sounds of the ocean all around her.

'Let's go celebrate in our new house,' she whispered as she reluctantly broke the kiss.

'Sounds good, any way of celebrating in mind?' Just the look in his eyes heated her through.

'I'm sure we can think of something,' she

promised as, hand in hand, they made their way back to their house. They'd come a long way over the last year and while she knew the future was always uncertain, as long as they were together, she knew she could face anything.

* * * * *

If you enjoyed this story,
check out these other great reads
from Jessica Gilmore

Miss Right All Along
It Started with a Vegas Wedding
Christmas with His Ballerina
The Princess and the Single Dad

All available now!

Get up to 4 Free Books!

We'll send you 2 free books from each series you try PLUS a free Mystery Gift.

FREE Value Over **$25**

Both the **Harlequin® Historical** and **Harlequin® Romance** series feature compelling novels filled with emotion and simmering romance.

YES! Please send me 2 FREE novels from the Harlequin Historical or Harlequin Romance series and my FREE Mystery Gift (gift is worth about $10 retail). After receiving them, if I don't wish to receive any more books, I can return the shipping statement marked "cancel." If I don't cancel, I will receive 5 brand-new Harlequin Historical books every month and be billed just $6.39 each in the U.S. or $7.19 each in Canada, or 4 brand-new Harlequin Romance Larger-Print books every month and be billed just $7.19 each in the U.S. or $7.99 each in Canada, a savings of 20% off the cover price. It's quite a bargain! Shipping and handling is just 50¢ per book in the U.S. and $1.25 per book in Canada.* I understand that accepting the 2 free books and gift places me under no obligation to buy anything. I can always return a shipment and cancel at any time by calling the number below. The free books and gift are mine to keep no matter what I decide.

Choose one: ☐ **Harlequin Historical**
(246/349 BPA G36Y)

☐ **Harlequin Romance Larger-Print**
(119/319 BPA G36Y)

☐ **Or Try Both!**
(246/349 & 119/319 BPA G36Z)

Name (please print)

Address   Apt. #

City   State/Province   Zip/Postal Code

Email: Please check this box ☐ if you would like to receive newsletters and promotional emails from Harlequin Enterprises ULC and its affiliates. You can unsubscribe anytime.

> Mail to the **Harlequin Reader Service:**
> **IN U.S.A.:** P.O. Box 1341, Buffalo, NY 14240-8531
> **IN CANADA:** P.O. Box 603, Fort Erie, Ontario L2A 5X3

Want to explore our other series or interested in ebooks? Visit www.ReaderService.com or call 1-800-873-8635.

HHHRLP25